GREEN GAUNTLET

A Don Lamplighter Christmas Special

Dean M. Lichterman

GREEN GAUNTLET

A Don Lamplighter Christmas Special

Dean M. Lichterman

Christian Publishing House
Professional Christian Publishing of the Good News!

ISBN-13: **978-0692593943**

ISBN-10: **0692593942**

Christian Publishing House

Cambridge, Ohio

GREEN GAUNTLET A Don Lamplighter Christmas Special by Dean M. Lichterman

Table of Contents

Acknowledgments

Thank you to my wife Lori for all of the work she put into the cover of both this and the last book "Cane & Able."

I also thank Pastor Doug Buchanan and my wife's aunt, Joanne Sawyer, for their help in the proofreading.

Chapter 1

"Ummm ... Hands up?" All Don Lamplighter could do was tilt his head to the left side in a quizzical manner when he heard the loud, unique demand outside of the local pharmacy.

"I said - Hands up!"

It was early Monday morning on Dec. 19 and Lamplighter was ringing bells for the Salvation Army. He was being confronted by a smallish young gentleman for what he surmised was a ridiculous reason that he was about to learn.

"Give me what's in the pot," demanded the man.

This was one of Lamplighter's busiest weeks of the year. With the economy as bad as it is - an unemployment rate of 15-percent – he has taken a paid job ringing bells to help his family afford the bills. He stands out in the cold 20 hours a week. This is in addition to his 32 hours a week at the Wal-Mart and his freelance writing assignments.

The week was tough on him, but the money was helpful.

"Are you deaf you fat slob?" said his attacker. "Give me the damn pot!"

The man stood about four inches shorter than the 5-foot-11 inch tall Lamplighter. Making the confrontation equalized was the fact that the shorter antagonist's hand was in his right pocket. It appeared he had a gun.

"Make up your mind, do you want my hands up, or do you want me to hand you the pot?" replied Lamplighter with a sigh of sarcasm.

Experience has taught Lamplighter to think ahead and be prepared for scenarios. He has been ringing bells for three Christmas seasons now and has mentally rehearsed what he would do if someone had attacked him for the money.

This one was different, however. He had developed plans for a physical confrontation, even when they had a gun. This one was so nervous that he made it seem like it was his first time attempting a robbery.

"Um... Um... Um... just give me the pot," replied the attacker.

The smallish attacker had planned out this situation in advance as well. All of the attacker's ideas had been simple - show like you have a gun and take the money. He had never imagined that he would run into a guy named Lamplighter, who would not be afraid.

"Don't you realize that this money is going to a charity to help others?" responded Lamplighter in a caring tone. "Are you that desperate for cash that you are willing to do that?"

"I.. I.. I.. I.. I don't care," stuttered the attacker. "I need the cash too."

The man, whom Lamplighter estimated to be in his early 20s, was dressed warmly, but in clothes that were well worn - a tattered gray sweatshirt with a black winter vest and blue jeans with holes in both knees.

"Well, since this money is going to a charity anyway," said Lamplighter, followed by a short pause. "Why don't you just go to a church and ask for help?"

He had tried this strategy before when propositioned by a prostitute. It didn't work then, but Lamplighter reasoned that since a possible outcome would be setting someone on the path toward accepting Christ, it was worth another shot. He also thought that by prolonging the confrontation, there would be more opportunity for either a pharmacy employee or another bystander to notice the situation and call the police.

"Just give me the pot," replied the attacker. "I have a gun you know."

That is when Lamplighter came to a realization. It was only 10 a.m. and he had been ringing for about an hour. That fact, combined with the blustery 10-degree temperature in Canandaigua, New York was keeping people away, led him to estimate that there was only about $10 in the pot anyway.

."Tell you what let's compromise," said Lamplighter.

"No compromise," shouted the attacker! "I want the pot!"

"Let's do this," offered Lamplighter as he rubbed his chin in deep thought.

"I'll keep my hands up and you can take the pot yourself."

The attacker hesitated but finally nodded in agreement.

Lamplighter had thought that he would just let him keep the pot. However, his opponent was as new to crime as he had thought. The attacker turned his back and put both of his hands down to grab the donation kettle.

This allowed Lamplighter the opportunity to tackle his overmatched foe, being about 100 pounds heavier it was easy for him to do.

"I guess you really don't have a gun," said Lamplighter.

Unfortunately, Lamplighter was wearing thick winter gloves which prevented him from getting a good grip and the attacker was able to wiggle away. Given Lamplighter's bad leg, he was unable to pursue. Just as he had hoped, a bystander, an elderly woman who was a customer in the store did see him tackle his attacker and call the police. Sheriff J.P. Cornell arrived at the pharmacy about one minute after the altercation.

"Lucky for you, it has been a while since I've seen you," said Sheriff Cornell. "That's actually a good thing," replied Lamplighter. Cornell and Lamplighter were referring to several previous adventures. The Sheriff had been the first on the scene after Lamplighter rescued an infant from a car accident in late June. He also intervened when Lamplighter was accosted by a pimp's goon and helped him thwart a kidnapping attempt at Wal-Mart.

The pair had worked together to solve a murder mystery surrounding the car accident. All of the events took place within one week. Then just one week later, the Sheriff came to the scene when Lamplighter intervened in a child prostitution ring. Lamplighter's life had been quiet and routine since then.

"So is this the start of another busy week for you?" asked Cornell.

"I hope not," responded Lamplighter with a large sigh. "With all of the jobs I have, this week is going to be busy enough as it is."

The elderly lady then approached the Sheriff.

"I only saw a little bit," said the lady, who noted that she was the one who had called the police. "I saw the other guy try to take the pot of money, the big guy there tackle him, and the little guy gets away."

"That's pretty much how it finished," added Lamplighter, who continued to explain to the Sheriff how the situation started.

"Did either of you get a description?" asked the Sheriff.

"He was about four inches shorter than I and pretty skinny, but he had a hood over his head and I didn't see his face," noted Lamplighter.

The witness concurred with Lamplighter but added that he ran off back toward Main Street. "Good catch," said Lamplighter to the lady.

Sheriff Cornell also complimented the witness but added, "It looks like we have another mystery on our hands. I hope it doesn't spiral out of control like last time."

Just then an older couple arrived, and since the donation kettle was still hanging in its proper place, they added a bunch of coins.

"Well, I have to get back to my job," said Lamplighter as he assumed his place next to the familiar red tripod. "Thank you and Merry Christmas!" he said to the couple.

"Merry Christmas to you," they responded.

The next hour was the same, with only about seven more donations. Lamplighter helped pass the time by singing Christmas carols. The workers at the pharmacy appreciated this because it put their customers in a better mood and they bought more merchandise. Lamplighter also liked it because it gave him the opportunity to sing.

He also liked the $9.00 per hour wage the church paid to watch the kettles during the times they could not get volunteers.

During his break, he placed the kettle behind the service desk and used the restroom. His favorite style of candy bar was in stock and Lamplighter could not refuse the temptation. While in line he found a purple convertible die-cast car in a stack of impulse items and started to run it up and down his arm. Lamplighter had a collection of small vehicles and this would make an excellent addition.

"Having fun?" asked the giggling clerk.

"I collect these," said a somewhat embarrassed Lamplighter, who grew red in the face. "That and my favorite color is purple."

He put the car down and purchased the candy bar.

"I like your singing, by the way," said the clerk. "God bless you," replied Lamplighter. "Thanks and Merry Christmas!"

That is when he noticed another black limousine. He couldn't see the license plate, but somehow knew it was Absalom, the local leader of a global satanic syndicate that held an enclave in a resort on the outskirts of town during that same infamous week in June.

"What is he doing here again," he thought.

Chapter 2

Lamplighter's instinct was right. Absalom was in the limo and making a return trip to Canandaigua.

"I like it here," said the villain in the back of his ride.

He was there to get ready for another satanic festival, the Winter Solstice. He selected the same resort that his organization had enjoyed for his late summer global enclave.

"I think I should buy some land here," said Absalom. "Good waterfront property."

The car was crowded as he was with all seven of his top captains.

"We could use another market push into Canandaigua," said Madam Stephanie, a middle-aged woman who was the head of the organization's prostitution ring. "We are trying to get my girls to take over this area anyway and, well, Don Lamplighter can't be everywhere."

Every captain nodded in agreement.

"I wonder what happened to that guy. Has anyone heard of him lately?" asked Steve, who was a city councilor in Rochester, a city of more than 300,000 people which is about a 45-minute drive northwest of Canandaigua. "It's part of my job to keep track of the news. He hasn't been anywhere."

He was right. Lamplighter's life had been relatively uneventful since his last meeting with Absalom. The two had first met in person back in June when Absalom went into the Canandaigua Wal-Mart just to do a quick interview to find out what Lamplighter knew. Absalom concluded that he didn't know anything about the organization. They met twice after that for chess games, once by chance and one game on purpose. Absalom won both times.

"I think you haven't been paying attention," replied Julius, who is in charge of the organization's drug trade. "I read all of the religious publications in the area. Lamplighter still writes for Maranatha Monthly. He wrote a story about a new Christian drug rehab program."

"And as you have noted, the more people Christians get off of drugs, the less profit for us," said Absalom as he pointed to Julius.

Absalom added that he has hired a friend to follow Lamplighter and make weekly reports. The limo had reached the intersection of Main Street and Highways 5 & 20. Absalom and his captains got a good view of Canandaigua Lake as they went by.

"I've read an article by him," added Vic, who was in charge of the muscle of the group. "It was an interesting piece about the effectiveness of vitamin supplements."

Gabrielle was a grifter whom the organization uses to set up its enemies for a fall. She was not taking part in the conversation and appeared to be daydreaming as she ran her finger in circles on the window.

"What about you Gabrielle?" asked Absalom. "Heard anything about Don Lamplighter?"

"No but I think about him a lot," Gabrielle replied. "I've seen pictures of him – and I sure would like to get my hands on him."

Loan shark planner James flashed her a smile of disbelief before theft ring leader Alexander gave Gabrielle a light smack across the back of the head.

The captains laughed.

"I don't deal with him at all in my department," noted Julius.

"But I do," replied Alexander. "He still works at Wal-Mart in Canandaigua. We still go there sometimes."

As per Absalom's orders, the driver took a cruise on the road that mirrors the top of the lake.

"This is the land that I want," said Absalom while looking over at Steve. "You are going to have to explain that eminent domain thing to me again sometime."

The limo turned into the same resort the group had used for the Winter Solstice party, it was decked out like a Christmas paradise with snow-lined trees covering the main road into the hotel. It was daylight so all of the unlit traditional secular holiday characters were visible.

"This looks like Christmas," said Gabrielle, who was still looking out the window, she was paying attention more since seeing the decorations.

'That's the idea," said Absalom. "Quite a few of the Christmas traditions that are thought to be Christian in nature are actually pagan in origin."

"And like we've said before, by promoting this type of holiday we take Christ out of Christmas," chimed in Julius. 'The less influence the Christians have, the more people are on drugs, and the more profit we make."

"So in a way, all of the Christmas money spent on these decorations is actually helping our bottom line," added Steve. "Good thing our council has not cut out Rochester's Christmas signs."

"I like the way all of you are starting to think," said Absalom as he took his traditional pose, his fingers interlocked and his head resting on his hands.

The group then left the limo and entered the main lobby.

"This looks like the seasonal selection of Wal-Mart," Alexander added.

Gabrielle returned the favor with a smack across his head.

"This is going to be fun," said Absalom.

Chapter 3

Snow started falling as Lamplighter got back from his break. He can't help it, every time that the snow begins, he must start singing.

"Oh the weather outside is frightful ....." he started as he put his kettle back in for donations.

Lucky for him, he was stationed at the local pharmacy today. The pharmacy had a roof covering the main entrance, so the snow did not land on him. The cold temperature was bad enough with a wet jacket it may not be even worth the pay to guard the bucket.

Lamplighter put up the tripod to hold the kettle.

"But ... well I'm outside and it's so delightful," continued Lamplighter.

He hooked the kettle onto a chain that hung from the tripod and placed a bag of salt on the bottom to prevent it from toppling over in the wind.

"And since I've got four hours to go," he sang as he placed the sign on top of the tripod.

"Let it snow, let it snow, let it snow," belted out Lamplighter to finish his made-up version of the popular tune.

He received a donation as soon as the kettle was put up.

"Well I see you make the rounds," said the middle-aged, professionally-dressed woman who was placing a $5 bill into the slot.

"You sing everywhere you go," noted the lady. "You are kind of hard to forget."

"I don't know if that's good or bad," replied Lamplighter.

"Considering I donate whenever I see you, I would say it was a good thing," the lady said as she walked into the store. "Thank you and Merry Christmas," shouted Lamplighter.

Years of experience as a bell ringer have taught him to be prepared for the weather. Lamplighter wore a pair of dress socks covered by a pair of athletic socks inside of his insulated boots. The weather report showed the 10-degree temperature which prompted him to wear a pair of jeans with black sweatpants over them. Had it been warmer, or had he been inside, he would just wear the jeans.

Lamplighter wore his longest shirt, one that extended nearly down to his thighs. It provided a windbreaker and covered up what he called "crucial areas" should it become necessary to pick up any money dropped on the concrete.

He wore a long sleeve Henley over the shirt and an insulated hooded jacket that both he and his wife Gloria call 'Big Blue.' He also wore two sets of gloves; on this inside was a set of thin knit brown ones that he used to grip things and on the outside was a thick pair that allowed his attacker to get away. A buzzing in his inside coat pocket made it necessary to take off the outer pair of gloves. He brought his cell phone to keep in contact with Gloria.

"Hi honey, I'm awake," said the text message from Gloria.

"Well, happy week before Christmas," replied Lamplighter, his knit gloves keeping him warm while allowing him enough dexterity to hit the buttons on his cell phone.

"Do you have enough coffee?" she asked in her second text.

"I have about an hour's worth left," replied Don.

Don had brought coffee from home to stay warm, but given the dehydrating effects of caffeine on the body he had also brought a bottle of water. The coffee was cold by now, but the water was so cold that Lamplighter could only sip it.

"I'll bring a refill. I'll be there in an hour, Mwa," texted Gloria.

"I look forward to it, Mwa," he replied.

There were just enough donators to keep Lamplighter's mind occupied. He estimated he received about $30 in donations for that hour. He was glad to see the familiar black Neon family car take a spot in the lot.

It was just the family's luck. Gloria had taken a second job at a convenience store to raise money to get the Neon fixed. They had both cars working for about a week before the gold Dodge Stratus developed a problem with its struts and the Lamplighters did not have enough money to fix it. Since they had the contingency plan in place for having one car, all they did was switch into the Neon with the Stratus now stuck in the parking lot of their apartment complex.

Gloria met him with a smile as he opened the door.

"I got you what you wanted and a little something else," she said, holding up a small brown bag.

"Look forward to it, but for now, I have to go in the building for a few minutes," replied Don as he locked the kettle in the car.

Upon his return, he found a small bowl of hot egg soup waiting for him. Gloria had already filled his covered coffee mug with a freshly-made concoction of instant coffee and instant hot chocolate. She also brought him another water bottle and some cookies.

They left that car on to give Don a place to warm up.

"I have a story for you," said Don as he explained how somebody had tried to steal the kettle.

"Wow the world is getting crazy!" exclaimed Gloria as she turned on the radio.

"Wow the world is getting crazy!" shouted Gregg Matzek, a radio talk show host to whom the couple had started listening on a daily basis.

They shared a good laugh before Don went back to sipping his soup.

"The F.B.I. will tell you that crime is going down, but my sources and anecdotal evidence says that is not true," continued Matzek.

"If I were home, I could use the home phone to call in right now," said Don.

"Yeah this makes a good story," added Gloria.

Don finished his soup and wolfed down the cookies with the help of a few sips of coffee. The Lamplighters then reviewed the plan for the cars. Gloria had to be at work at 2 p.m. Don would finish at 3 p.m., walk to Gloria's store to get the car, go home and take a nap, shower and grab a quick bite. He then needed to head off to Victor for his writing assignment at the town board meeting.

Once finished there, Don would pick up his wife at her store. She usually ended her shift around 9:30 p.m. and she probably would have to wait in the store for him. They kissed as she left to get ready for work.

"I got one for you. Me, you and Gregg Matzek," said Gloria to start the couple's favorite word game - triples.

"I was thinking the same thing," said Don. "Three people who think that the world is going crazy."

"Well," replied Gloria. "Great minds think alike."

It was now 1 p.m. A Salvation Army captain Dave Irving was slated to pick him up at 3 p.m. Lamplighter actually looked forward to the next two hours - an excuse to sing more Christmas carols.

"I know you from the grocery store last year," said a military veteran who donated a handful of change. "You are the guy that sings."

"Yeah it makes the time go by," replied Lamplighter. "Plus I find it encourages people to donate."

"Well, how about Silent Night?' asked the veteran.

"I can do that," said Lamplighter, who just sang the first verse.

A crowd had gathered. Just that one song brought in $20 in donations.

When the captain arrived with his replacement, Lamplighter told him about the mugger.

"You should have called us right away," said the captain.

26

"Yeah, but I saved the kettle and stayed safe," noted Lamplighter.

"You should have just let him take it," noted the Captain.

"I actually tried to do that, but he turned his back on me and I took the opportunity," explained Lamplighter. "I also told him to go to the church for help."

"Well that was a good move," replied the captain.

"Too bad it didn't work," sighed Lamplighter; "but - speaking of help - can you please take me to get our car at Gloria's store?"

"Hop in," said that captain as he opened the sliding door for Lamplighter.

They used the time on the short drive to arrange a pick up for the next morning and discuss Lamplighter used the time to quietly reflect on his Bible study from that morning. He started January 1 with the first five chapters of Genesis and finished on November 20 with the last chapter of Revelation. Lamplighter has since taken up topical studies. This morning, he started passages regarding Christmas, starting with Isaiah 7, which includes the prophecy of Christ's birth. Of special importance was Verse 14 "Therefore the Lord himself shall give you a sign, behold a virgin shall conceive and bear a son and shall call his name Immanuel."

Lamplighter kissed Gloria outside her store before taking the car and heading home to rest up for the board meeting.

Chapter 4

It has been said that there is no rest for the wicked, so while Don Lamplighter was taking his break between jobs, Jacob Glass was taking, what he thinks is his second job up another step.

Glass is a crystal meth user. His plan to support his habit during the Christmas season is to steal Salvation Army donation kettles.

"It was simple, so simple," Glass said as he stomped around his apartment. "It seemed so easy - just run up and take the kettle."

He liked to watch the news on the 24-hour channel, but became even more disturbed when the newscaster started talking about him, even before the presidential election, crime in other cities and Middle Eastern wars. This is where he learned that the person he threatened earlier in the day was Don Lamplighter.

"Why did I pick the one kettle being watched by that guy" Glass muttered as he walked around in circles.

Glass did have a job working full time at a local deli that was barely enough to pay his bills so he took to petty crimes to support his drug habit.

"How could I have picked that one, how could I have picked that one!" yelled Glass as he continued to walk around and around his apartment. He was taking a clockwise direction and running his fingers through his hair.

There was a bell ringer outside of the deli, but he decided that it would be too risky there since people knew him. He also reasoned that it would be too difficult at Wal-Mart with all of the people there. The grocery store on the north side of town has an area inside where the bell is kept. Since he would have to wait for the door to open, it would not make for a fast getaway.

The plan then became to get them from what he considered soft targets. Glass would try to take the kettles from the pharmacy and a national drug store on the other end of the city.

Glass sat on his run-down couch. "I have to make the odds back in my favor," he thought to himself.

Glass then resumed stomping around the apartment, this time he was moving counterclockwise.

"How do I stop Don Lamplighter? How do I stop Don Lamplighter?" his muttering continued as well.

He only stopped to sit for about two seconds. Glass stood still and perfectly quiet then shouted while running his fingers through his hair.

"AAAAAAAAAHHHHHHHH" he screamed.

Glass jumped up and starting stomping around his apartment, again changing directions, back to clockwise.

The ideas started flowing. Should he try to just shoot him?

"I like that idea," he thought to himself. "But I don't even have a gun. That could complicate things."

The stomping and muttering continued. The next idea popped into his head. He considered taking Lamplighter out at Wal-Mart or someplace else.

"He is bigger than me and he proved that he can fight," he thought. "Not a good idea."

Lamplighter was close to his estimate of the size of Glass. He was 5-foot-6 and weighed 135 pounds.

Glass had again decided to attack Lamplighter and continued to think of a way as he stomped around his apartment - this time counter-clockwise again.

Then he suddenly stopped.

"Maybe I should just avoid Don Lamplighter?" he stood in the same spot for a good five minutes.

"That is not a bad idea I do have a car," he said with a shrug as he looked out the window at his black four-door Dodge Neon, the same year as Lamplighters.

He continued standing for another five minutes. Glass liked the idea of expanding his range of targets, but then decided that he still wanted to humiliate Lamplighter.

On that note, he continued walking.

"How do I get Don Lamplighter? How do I get Don Lamplighter?" around and around he continued until seeing a pair of green winter gloves that were left there by an old roommate.

If he didn't have a weapon, he decided to make one based around the green gloves.

Glass placed the gloves on the coffee table and stared at them with his head in his hands in a pose eerily similar to that of Lamplighter's other enemy - Absalom.

To decide what to add to it, he got up and walked around his apartment again. Now that he had an idea, the walk changed from a stomp to a quiet search for items to attach to the gloves to make a tough weapon. He found thumb tacks on a small desk he had in a corner next to them was enough rubber cement to attach them to the gloves.

He sat on the couch to glue together what Glass thought would be his masterpiece.

"This should do the trick," he thought to himself after taking a swift whiff of the adhesive.

But fighting Lamplighter would probably require more firepower and thus he took another walk around his apartment, he found pepper spray that was actually used on him by a young woman he brought here to share some drugs. Another look out the window at his car gave him the second idea. He would grab a couple of the sticks and use them as a striking weapon as well.

"This completes it," Glass thought to himself.

He then had another thought.

"I should test them first before trying everything out on Lamplighter," he said to himself. Glass fell back asleep for several hours. When he awoke, he went out to his car, sat in the driver's seat and thought about where he would go. He thought of the perfect spot.

"I've scouted out the Clock Family Grocery store in Victor and they do have a kettle there," Glass said with a sigh as he started the car.

He got to Clock. The theft went as easy as clockwork. Glass waited for the area to be free of customers and walked up to the smallish, elderly-looking man ringing the bell. Glass conked him on the head with the stick, grabbed the kettle, ran back to his car and drove off with the loot. "Yes!" he said.

The whole process took two hours, starting with the walks around his apartment at 4 p.m. and leaving the Clock Family Grocery store at 6 p.m.

Glass, a career criminal, was able to find an isolated spot in an industrial park in Canandaigua to pick the lock on the kettle and get the loot. He counted about $200, yet there was an unsatisfying feeling. He knew from experience that the stick worked, but he didn't get a chance to throw a punch while wearing his new gloves.

"I'll just have to do this again," he said with a smile.

Chapter 5

"Here is the trick," said Dr. Joe Hammill while Don Lamplighter turned on his car radio. "The strategy from their own words is this - pretend to be nice, take over the political movements and trick people into accepting the agenda. This doesn't mean that the average person that agrees with those words is a bad person, it only means they believe a lie, or several lies."

Lamplighter was on his way to another Victor town board meeting.

It was the first meeting after the annual budget was approved, so he didn't expect the gathering to get too heated. He got a look at the agenda through the town's website.

"It doesn't look too bad," he said as he drove through the parking lot of his apartment complex. "But then again, I've thought that before and ended up sitting there for four hours."

Lamplighter started the traditional route to the meeting. He had done the check before he left and all of his supplies were with him - digital recorder, digital camera, notebook and two pens. He also had his homemade mug of coffee and a bottle of water. Just to make sure he also brought a handful of cough drops to counter his lengthy sneezing attacks.

"A good example of this is the so called green agenda," noted Dr. Hammill as his show came back from commercial as Lamplighter took a right-hand turn onto Main Street.

'There are good things about it, such as recycling and the pursuit of alternative energy and the growing of different types of plants," said Hammill. "But they add other things like this whole cap-and-trade system which only adds more money to the pockets of the global elite."

Lamplighter was stopped at the light at the north end of town. Whenever he and Gloria are riding around in the Neon, they play a game where they wave to every other Neon that they see. It was homage to the commercial that introduced the product.

This time there was a Neon waiting to go south at the same light. Lamplighter waved and as usual, he didn't get anything back. This time there was a reason - he didn't know it, but he had just acknowledged Jacob Glass, who was on his way back from taking the kettle from the Clock Family grocery in Victor.

Lamplighter did however get a jolt from the next statement from the radio.

"One of those groups is the Global Environmental Initiative," said Dr. Joe Hammill.

He left the light with a new found interest in the upcoming meeting as a speaker from the Global

Environmental Initiative was on the agenda. Lamplighter turned up the volume and listened intently.

"What they do is get a city council to claim eminent domain on a particular piece of land," continued Dr. Hammill. "Then once that happens, they take over the land and sell it to their friends at a huge profit. Then, they tax other people's land to give the money to themselves."

He had a guest who was fighting the group's incursion into Spokane, WA. It is one of the cities where people were gathering in large numbers to protest the group's actions.

"The worst part of this is that the municipalities pay them $600 per month to do it," said the guest, a retired teacher. "This is all done in the name of sustainable development."

"I've heard that term before," Lamplighter thought to himself "pretty much every time that I go to a meeting."

"The things that the GEI has on its website are frightening - everything from controlling human population to using the environment to enact what it calls an anti-poverty agenda, even though it will just give more power to the elite," continued the host.

The show went to commercial as Lamplighter was passed by a limo. He was driving on a four-lane road, sticking to the right since he was driving a vehicle that was now 11 years old and he and his wife have had bad luck with cars.

It didn't take long for the limo driver to make his move, but Lamplighter still had time to catch the license plate - Gambit. He was just passed by Absalom, but since it was the first time that they met while Lamplighter was driving the Neon, he figured the odds-on bet is that he would not be recognized by his rival.

"Exactly where are we going?" asked Madam Stephanie as the limo passed by.

It was headed away from the resort.

"We are going to the Victor town board meeting," said Absalom.

Six of the seven department captains were in the limo, noted by his absence was Steve, who left earlier in a different vehicle so he could get to his own city council meeting in Rochester. All six had a confused look on their faces.

"OK, I'll ask," chimed in Julius. "Why are we going there?"

"To make sure everything goes to plan," said Absalom. "I have been asked to do a favor by a friend of mine; well a friend of ours."

The limo sped away fast enough, but the traffic on the highway was as crowded as usual so it couldn't get out of Lamplighter's sight.

"I wonder where they are going?" Lamplighter asked himself.

Dr. Joe Hammill came back from the break as the limo, followed by two cars and then Lamplighter continued down the highway. The four cars came to a stop at the light to make the left-hand turn on the road that eventually turns into main street, Victor.

"Think globally act locally," said Hammill. "That is a great sounding slogan, but what it really is, is a way to trick people into accepting this evil agenda."

"As a state governor once said 'we couldn't get it passed at the federal level, so we are going to get it passed at the local level,'" said the guest. "So I encourage everyone to go to their local council and fight this."

Lamplighter was looking forward to hearing what GEI had to say, but he ran into a problem - the limo that he was tailing turned into the town hall parking lot. In front of the building was a group of protesters holding signs demanding changes to the tax code.

"I can't let Absalom see me in this car," Lamplighter thought to himself. "But those protesters do give me another story idea."

He decided to drive by and wait in the lot of a pharmacy a couple of blocks away. It also gave him the opportunity to listen to the radio show and learn more about the GEI.

"Their agenda is terrible," said the guest. "You can check it out for yourself at the website www.GEI.com."

'That is easy to remember," said Lamplighter. "I will have to check it out."

"And always remember," added Dr. Joe Hammill. "There is a spiritual aspect to this as the people pushing the agenda are motivated to take over the world to serve the dark lord that they worship".

"That is what concerns me," Lamplighter thought. "Now I have to go to a board meeting and look them right in the face ...... come to think of it, I look forward to this."

Chapter 6

Glass was happy that he was suddenly $200 richer but quickly realized that it was not going to be enough to support his meth habit for as long as he had hoped.

"$200, that's it!" he screamed. "News reports weren't kidding, people are donating less in the recession."

He had hoped to get enough from just one score to support his drug habit for at least a couple of months. Feeling desperate, he began looking around his house for loose change.

Glass started his nervous routine all over again. He got up off the couch and around and around the apartment he went.

"I'm going to have to do this again," he said as he stopped with a smile.

Just as soon as he stopped, he started his nervous stomp.

"I'm going to have to do this again," he muttered as he took his tour at an ever increasing speed.

Eventually, he became so dizzy that he needed to sit on his couch. This provided Glass the opportunity to scrounge for extra money in the couch cushions.

"With all of the drug addicts that crash on here there has to be at least some extra cash in these," he said aloud to nobody.

Stomping around the room made him very hungry. His apartment was right downtown, within walking distance of Gloria's store.

"Hmmmm junk food yeahhhhhhh," he said with a drool as he walked into the store.

"Oh great that guy is back in here," noted Gloria, who is the acting manager of the store, to the two other employees there at the time. "We have to watch out for him."

Glass took a slow walk around the food section. There was a small selection of frozen foods and no fresh produce in the store, but it did have five aisles of packaged edibles and three rows of special Christmas treats of cookies and chocolate. Since he didn't want to cook, this was the perfect place to get food.

However, the store did not have his favorite brand of cookie in stock.

"What the hell is wrong with this damn store?" he said within the audible range of a father with two preteen girls in tow.

"Hey watch your language, there are kids here," said the father.

Glass just gave a dirty look, mumbled something unintelligible and looked for the cookies.

After going through the selections twice, Glass, who was not paying attention to where he was going, bumped into a customer - a 30-year-old woman with two children. The customer called over one of the employees - an 18-year-old male, Jim, who was working at his first job. The employee saw Glass place an item in his pocket.

Gloria was alerted.

"Excuse me," Gloria said to Glass. "I have had some complaints about you and I'm afraid that I am going to have to ask you to leave the store."

"Awww, come on man," slurred Glass. "I didn't do nothin'."

"Well you bumped into one customer, I have had one employee say that you put something in your pocket and well ... you have an offensive odor," replied Gloria with the male employee behind her for security. "Could you please leave our store?"

"I want to leave anyway," screamed Glass. "This store is a piece of garbage that doesn't even have my favorite brand of cookies."

The father turned the corner to confront Glass again only to see Gloria and Jim already attempting to control the situation.

"Hey, you watch your language in here. This is a family store," she said in a stern voice. "I've told you once, you need to leave now or I will have to call the police."

Glass saw both Jim and the father behind Gloria and shrugged his shoulders; "Whatever duuuude," he said quietly as he turned to walk out of the store. Jim followed with Gloria and the father watching to make sure that he actually left.

"This store is crap!" he yelled as he walked out the door.

"I don't envy you working here with all of the people that you get in this store," said the mother.

"Well, I appreciate that you try to keep a clean environment for my kids," added the father.

"Thank you, I try to keep this as a family store and I have to look out for my customers," said Gloria.

Glass got to his apartment, his hands empty without food. He started to punch his hands together.

"I guess I have to add another enemy to my list," said Glass and fell asleep.

Chapter 7

Don Lamplighter has not seen Absalom in person since July 5th but he has thought about him every day. What is Absalom up to? When is it going to happen? How does that affect his family?

"Watch," he thought. "He and his group have their hands all over GEI."

The radio shows to which Lamplighter listens give information and predictions, some correct and some not, about the future. Some of this makes sense to him, some of it does not. Mainstream news confirms much of what they say and some of the meetings that Lamplighter attends parallel the thoughts of the radio announcers, which gives him food for thought.

"I wonder if today is going to give me another clue," said Lamplighter to himself as he pulled into the parking lot of town hall. "And by the way, the temperature is 20 degrees, why should I keep drinking iced coffee? Hot coffee would make more sense and it's cheaper since I don't have to add milk and hot chocolate - just good old hot coffee."

Lamplighter took a look around as he pulled into the Victor Town Hall parking lot. He was almost late for the meeting, but he still took the time to spot the black limo. Lamplighter decided to park on the other side of an SUV in case anyone was still in the limo who could spot him coming out of what he hoped was an unknown car. Since he usually stayed late for interviews and to review his notes, Lamplighter surmised that the limo would leave before he would and he would be safe.

"Whew!" Lamplighter made a deep sigh as he collected his equipment: "two pens, check; recorder, check; notebook, check; printed agenda, check."

He grabbed his cane and left the car for the walk to the building. He didn't know what he was going to look forward to more ... seeing Absalom again or finding confirmation of the GEI.

Lamplighter opened the doors to the meeting room. With the exception of Absalom and his squad of minions, it was the same as any other meeting.

The building was built just one year ago and it showed its modern amenities. To Lamplighter's left was the projection screen used for presentations and to show the audience the agenda. The audience was bigger at these meetings compared to the village's sessions. The seating capacity of the room approached 200 and the room was typically filled to half of that. The public had a chance to speak at the meeting during two public comment sessions.

To prepare for this, Victor supplied a microphone and podium. This made Lamplighter's job a lot easier. The speakers were required by the council to clearly identify themselves so he could track them down after the meeting, and being highly audible made it easier to take notes. Each member of the board had their own microphone as well.

The council was at full quorum for this meeting. To Lamplighter's left were the Democrats, Mark Cavanaugh, and Pete McDermott, both retired businessmen. Next was the apolitical town clerk, a young woman named Jill O'Brian. In the middle was Victor Town Supervisor Jeff Lyons, a tall man in his later 40's who had recently won a special election. The attorney seat was to Lyons's left. A law firm was contracted to fill the seat on a rotational bases, with tonight's lucky winner being a female named Amy Connors whom Lamplighter had never met.

Republicans occupied the two council spots on Lamplighter's right - Lawrence Ried, a golf club owner in his later 50s and John Cooper, a 35-year-old factory worker. Lyons was also a Republican, leaving that party with a 3-2 advantage on votes.

"OK here we go," Lamplighter thought to himself as he entered the room.

He spotted the usual crowd of department heads, people that were there to argue about an environmentally sensitive area, those who spoke out on the budget last time and a group of students who were there as a class requirement. The familiar faces made it easy for him to locate Absalom, who was in his public persona as banker Ken Knight. He was there with one woman, Gabrielle whom Lamplighter remembered from her exploratory trip to Wal-Mart last June. The rest of his captains had already left in waiting cars. Lamplighter also noticed Randall Meyer, who is the leader of Victor's "Green

Team" and the spokesperson who introduced GEI to both the village and the township.

Lamplighter took his customary place in the room. He sat one seat in and one seat back from the front. This allowed him an empty chair for his cane and any papers that he might get during the meeting. It also put him right next to the podium so he could hand his card to any speakers whom he might find newsworthy.

He set down his reporter's tools and tried to text Gloria that he had arrived at the meeting, but was stopped mid-text to say the Pledge of Allegiance, which was led by Lyons.

"Got here just in time," Lyons said to Lamplighter after the pledge to a quick chuckle from the crowd.

Lamplighter just smiled and finished his text.

In the front two rows opposite the podium sat the protesters. They didn't have their signs but were easily identified by their T-shirts. They were white with green lettering saying "No Sustainable Tax".

After opening the meeting with the Pledge, Supervisor Lyons pointed out the room's emergency exits, as per New York State Law.

The meeting progressed as usual with the approval of the minutes of the previous meeting, and the list of bills that were paid over that time frame. Next, it was time for the public comments. The protesters lined up to speak.

The first was an older gentleman named Steve Clive. He gave a history of the Sustainable Tax. Lamplighter learned that it was enacted as part of a "Green Team" plan that was approved by the board two years ago and scheduled to be in effect January 1.

"I urge you to repeal the tax", finished the speaker.

Lamplighter was embarrassed he didn't know of the tax sooner. He took notes for his story. He recognized the second speaker, a woman, as an accountant who practiced in the village. She spoke regarding the tax's impact on the community. She especially showed concern for the older citizens who owned larger properties.

The third speaker was a shorter male whom Lamplighter did not recognize. He told the council and the audience about the history of GEI including that other cities are fighting against it.

"Wow," mumbled Lamplighter – "quite the newsy night."

The fourth speaker approached the podium. He looked to be the same height as Lamplighter but appeared to be in much better shape, like that of a young military veteran.

"I'm going to make this shorter than my fellow protesters," he said.

The man then pulled a gun from his waist and took aim at Cavanaugh, who took a lethal shot to the middle of the forehead. Lamplighter put down his coffee as a quick second shot hit its mark through McDermott's gaping mouth.

Lamplighter jumped to intervene, but the shooter took the other side of the podium, effectively blocking himself from Lamplighter. He grazed O'Brian in the ear as she tried to duck and Lyons in the top of the head before the supervisor attempted to shield himself with a chair.

The assailant headed for the emergency exit further away from Lamplighter. The move around the podium gave him a big enough lead to get a shot off at Connors, hitting her in the shoulder. Lamplighter fell further behind the shooter as his bad leg prevented him from getting up a good head of steam.

Cooper was able to duck in time to avoid a shot. The shooter was able to get a bead on Reid as he got to the door, connecting with a bullet into his torso. The shooter made his way outside.

Lamplighter continued his slow pursuit but stopped in his tracks at the emergency exit as the assailant turned the gun on him. Lamplighter dove to the side, hearing two shots. He didn't feel any pain and didn't find any blood around him, so Lamplighter got back up and peeked outside. Standing above the protestor were both Absalom's bodyguard and a man Lamplighter thought was Absalom's driver.

Lamplighter was left with one foot outside and one inside. He surveyed the scene, wondering what to do next.

Chapter 8

Lamplighter's first thought was to call 911, but judging from the appearance of two sheriff vehicles there was no need for that.

Still reaching for his cell phone, he sent a text message to his wife.

"There was a shooting here, but I am OK. I will tell you later," it said.

The next was to the editor of the Victor News.

'There was a shooting here at the council," it read. "Please hold paper for the late story."

Lamplighter then headed to the council to render aid to the victims. He heard screams from Cavanaugh's wife as she held what appeared to be his lifeless body. McDermott's corpse was nearby, covered by a jacket. Deputy town clerk Katie Laurel was holding the wrist of O'Brian.

Lyons' body provided the most gruesome view as the bullet took off the top of his head. His body was prone with the chair on top of it. Connors was delicately walking away from the scene. She was clutching her bleeding shoulder as Cooper and recreation department manager Gerald Crosby helped her to a nearby table where a protester was opening a first-aid kit.

Reid's wife and daughter were sobbing as they embraced near his body.

Seeing that he could offer no additional help, Lamplighter grabbed his camera and recorder to get the story. Just then his phone started vibrating. It was a text from his editor.

"Get what you can. I will combine it with any press release," replied his editor. "Also get tasteful photos. Thanks."

Lamplighter got to work.

"OK, let's see what I can do," he sighed.

Doing his best to avoid any dead bodies in photos, he first aimed at the Reid family embrace, which now grew to four with the addition of two more of his adult children. He next got a series of photos of the protester, Cooper and a bystander helping with Connors.

Cooper noticed and approached Lamplighter.

"Look, I know that you are just trying to do your job here, but I think you should respect the victims and their families," he said, "especially this close to Christmas."

"Don't worry, of course, I will," replied Lamplighter.

Cooper turned away, then turned around and faced Lamplighter.

"I would like to make a statement," he said.

Lamplighter got out his recorder to catch Cooper speaking on behalf of the town of Victor and offering condolences to the victims and their families. Cooper then turned to a grateful hug from his wife.

Lamplighter then took pictures of a group of about 15 people in a prayer circle.

"Ahem," coughed a male voice behind him.

It was the first protester who spoke that evening.

"You are Don Lamplighter correct?" he asked. Lamplighter nodded.

"I would also like to make a statement," he said with tears flowing from both eyes.

Lamplighter switched on the recorder as the protester, who again introduced himself as Steve Clive, the leader of the protesters.

He too offered his thoughts and prayers to the victims but was interrupted by a punch to the face from another member of the audience.

"This is your fault," said the man. "You and your stupid group are causing all of the problems in the village."

The man was instantly arrested by a Sheriff Deputy.

"I don't have anything left to say," Clive said as he walked away.

Lamplighter then went outside to get a few images of some Sheriff's Department members collecting evidence from the scene. He tried to get an interview with one of Absalom's guards but was quickly spurned by his arch enemy.

"These guys have nothing to say to you Lamplighter," said Absalom. "I am going to speak for them. I am here to learn about the resolution to allow the rezoning of a property to allow one of my bank branches to open."

Absalom grinned as he continued.

"I feared for my life as well as the lives of everyone in the room as the shots started going off. I am proud of my bodyguards for their quick actions," he said. "They saved many lives today."

Lamplighter was disgusted. He thanked Absalom for his comments while pondering what he was up to.

Sheriff J.P. Cornell waited for his turn.

"OK," he said to Lamplighter. "Let's hear your side of the story."

Lamplighter described the events in detail before turning his recorder on the sheriff.

"OK," noted Lamplighter with a slight frown "your turn."

Lamplighter sat to write down the timetable of events from his perspective in order to write a proper story. He looked up to see Clive talking to another protester.

Lamplighter walked over to exchange business cards.

"Now is not a good time, but I would like to know more about what you are protesting," started Lamplighter. "I will be in Farmington tomorrow for a 7 p.m. meeting. Want to meet after that?"

"Sounds good," said Clive. "How about 8:30 at Dunkin Donuts on 332?"

"One of my favorites," said Lamplighter before he was rudely interrupted by a State Police officer dressed in riot gear.

"Get over against that wall," he yelled at Clive.

Lamplighter noticed that all of the remaining protesters were being herded and searched.

"I don't know what you are you are up to, but we will stop you!" shouted the leader of the State Police team. He then pointed to Lamplighter. "And you!" he barked. "Put that thing away."

Lamplighter shrugged as he sat to collect himself. Despite all of the action, it was only 8 p.m., leaving him time to get home and work on the story before having to pick up Gloria from her store at 9:30.

He tracked down Cornell just before he left.

"You know where to find me," said Lamplighter as he walked to his car, making sure that he had his reporter equipment with him.

He texted his wife to make sure that she knew of his plan before heading back home.

Chapter 9

"Hey boss, guess who I just saw," said Absalom's driver as he opened the door for his boss to get into to the black limo.

The driver had been in Absalom's employ since June. To keep his secret identity, Absalom has hired one driver and one bodyguard crew for each of his dual identities.

"Well?" Absalom asked as he entered the vehicle. Gabrielle stood nearby waiting her turn.

"Don Lamplighter," noted the driver.

"I don't see how this is a big deal," added Gabrielle as she took her turn getting into the car. "We just saw him in there and he acted like he didn't even know us."

"I caught that too," replied Absalom. "But for our plan to work, he is necessary."

Gabrielle gave him a quizzical look.

"Or at least for this part," continued Absalom, "or my next chess victory. I beat him twice you know."

"But he didn't get here in a gold car," replied the driver through the intercom.

"OK, tell me," ordered Absalom in a frustrated voice as he nodded his head toward the driver's seat.

"This might be why we thought we haven't heard from him," whispered Gabrielle. "Are we looking for the wrong car?"

"That's what worries me," said Absalom as he assumed his traditional pose - elbows on his knees, fingers interlocked and head rested on hands.

"Lamplighter got here in a black Dodge Neon," said the driver.

"Any reason why you haven't told me this yet?" asked Absalom.

"I just saw it today as he was getting into the parking lot tonight after you went into the town hall," said the driver.

"That does sound like a plausible excuse," replied Absalom. "Take us back to the compound."

Absalom and Gabrielle just stared at each other as the car left the town hall parking lot, headed for Rochester.

"I wonder how I missed that?" asked Absalom to himself, but audible enough for Gabrielle to hear.

"Maybe it's not even his car," said Gabrielle. "Or he could have purchased it after we did a search for the gold car."

"All possibilities," noted Absalom, still in his thinking pose. "I have to do a computer search when we get back to the compound."

"You enjoy that stuff," noted Gabrielle.

Absalom laughed. "I guess I should thank him for that."

He then hit the intercom button.

"Driver?" asked Absalom. "Did you happen to write down a license plate number of the car?"

"Yeah I got it right here," said the driver.

Absalom leaned over to Gabrielle.

"Get your cell phone out," Absalom said as he hit the intercom button again.

"OK driver tell us what it is," Absalom commanded.

"DML 1052," said the driver.

"You got that?" Absalom asked Gabrielle.

"Yep," she replied as she showed her cell phone screen to her captain.

"Good job driver," said Absalom as he turned on the intercom yet again. "Pick a restaurant, go to the drive through and get what you want. Add two vanilla milkshakes to that."

Absalom then checked the news on his laptop. He has a special assignment from the global syndicate to help steal the election for their chosen candidate. Absalom is working on the project, but is having some difficulty with the amount of candidates - at last count 11 Republican and 5 Democrats - to scandal out of the race.

"You always listen to the news," pouted Gabrielle as she sat back into her seat.

"The better to invest your money my dear," replied Absalom as he kissed Gabrielle's hand.

Lamplighter got back in his car at 8:20 p.m., about 15 minutes after Absalom and his crew left the town hall.

"Well that was eventful," Lamplighter thought to himself. "I have quite a bit of work to do now."

The time left him a wide window to pick up Gloria. Her store closes at 9 p.m. and she spends a half hour afterward to clean. It is about a 20-minute drive back to Canandaigua. That allowed him to go home first and work on deadline.

"OK where should I start?" Lamplighter thought about his story while driving down the main highway back to the city.

The traffic was pretty heavy on the street, leaving Lamplighter time to pick the radio station for the trip home. A talk show that he liked did not start until 9 p.m. so the choice for tonight was a gospel station.

"Perfect for this occasion," Lamplighter thought to himself.

Absalom was still listening to the news. "Salvation Army bell ringers in both Canandaigua and Victor were attacked today by somebody fitting the same description," said the newscaster.

"What a moron," noted Absalom. "High risk getting caught, low return, there can't be that much money in those kettles."

He stopped and thought for a moment.

"Still that is pretty brazen," he made a note on his laptop to call his captains and find out who the thief was. "He might be useful."

"The Sheriff's Department spokesman lists the assailant as a white male 5-6 and 135 pounds", continued the voice on the radio.

"Is he talking about you?" Gabrielle laughed.

"Heck no, I'm way smarter than that," replied Absalom in a somewhat angry manner. "That's why I help banks rob people electronically."

"Sorry," said Gabrielle as she bowed her head in shame.

"He was seen wearing a grey hooded sweatshirt and black winter vest," added the newscaster.

"Besides I'm 5-8," laughed Absalom as he listened passively.

"A witness claims that the first person attacked was Don Lamplighter, who was able to keep the attacker from getting the kettle," reported the newscaster.

Absalom perked up.

"The Sheriff's Department is looking for a black Neon with the first letter of the license plate 'D'," said the newscaster to finish the report.

Absalom picked up his phone and dialed 911. He described the car and gave the sheriff the location - the main road in Victor and laughed.

"Aren't you worried about getting caught with a cell phone trace like they found Pastor Joe in our compound?" asked Gabrielle.

"Good question," noted Absalom. "However, I am in my Knight character tonight. The phone is connected to him. Besides, people already saw me at the Victor meeting. Even if I am wrong, it will add to my concerned citizen persona."

Lamplighter was on that road. He reached the point where he had rescued the baby in June. Lamplighter still gets a pit in his stomach whenever he drives past the intersection. This time he had a different reason; the lights of a sheriff's car behind him.

He pulled over to the side of the road. The deputy approached with a gun drawn on Lamplighter.

"Drop the keys out of the window and keep your hands where I can see them," said the deputy.

Lamplighter was confused, but calmly complied.

The sheriff approached and got close enough to identify Lamplighter.

"It's just you," laughed the deputy as he put his gun back into its holster. "Sorry about that."

Lamplighter looked outside to see the face of deputy Josh Bultmant, who had helped Lamplighter when he was attacked outside of a Wal-Mart store several months back.

"About what was all of that?" asked Lamplighter.

Deputy Bultmant explained that the department got a tip that the vehicle matching the description of the kettle thief was around.

"So I was pulled over because someone thought I was the guy that attacked me?" questioned Lamplighter.

"I apologize for that," said Deputy Bultmant as he picked up and handed Lamplighter his keys. You are free to go."

Lamplighter pulled away as Bultmant got into his car and radioed the incident to dispatchers, noting that the license plate belonged to Lamplighter's car.

"That guy talks funny," Bultmant said aloud as he went back to his office in Victor.

The rest of Lamplighter's trip back to Canandaigua was uneventful, but filled with enjoyable music. He made it home to start his computer, upload the photos and translate his recorder. There was one message on his answering machine. It was from his father saying "Merry Christmas." Lamplighter's dad lives in Wisconsin. They try to talk by phone at least once every two weeks.

"I guess I am it," he thought as he dialed his dad's number.

After eight rings, he hung up and left to pick up Gloria. He pulled up to Gloria's store just as she was locking the door, Jim was with her.

About time you got here," said Gloria as she was getting into the car.

"Sorry, working on my story," replied Lamplighter as they watched Jim leave the parking lot in his own vehicle. "Oh and check this out, apparently our Neon looks like the car of the guy who tried to take the kettle away from me this morning,"

"Wow that's frightening," noted Gloria as they left the parking lot.

On the way home she explained how she had to kick somebody out of the store that day.

As soon as the couple got home, Lamplighter went up to the office to finish and send the story and photos about the shooting.

True to his custom, the couple's night Bible study was decided by randomly flipping through a book containing Psalms, Proverbs and the New Testament. He then read the verses on those two pages. He landed on Psalm 78, which is a review of how the Hebrews doubted God despite their escape from slavery in Egypt. According to verse 32, "In spite of this they still sinned, and did not believe in his wondrous works."

It reminded him of what he perceived as a rejection of Christmas.

"That is what happens when people don't think they need God," he said with a shrug.

Don came down at 11 p.m. and ate a pizza while enjoying a good spy movie with Gloria before heading to bed at around 1 a.m.

"A surprise, surprise and surprise," said Gloria to start a game of triples, which was a technique the Lamplighters use to relax.

Don thought for a second "Oh three things you got me for Christmas."

Gloria turned to Don and smiled.

Chapter 10

"Interesting circle you have started," said Lamplighter to the middle-aged woman who gave a donation to the kettle while she was entering the drug store.

"I don't understand." said the woman who looked quizzically at Lamplighter.

Lamplighter was not surprised that he was not recognized. Tuesday was even colder than Monday, so he added a scarf to his wardrobe for ringing bells.

He had just gotten there to set up after being dropped off by the Captain Irving. Lamplighter had just placed his coffee and water bottle on the ground under the famous red tripod and put up his scarf before the woman had made her donation.

"Well you just put money in the kettle," noted Lamplighter.

"But how does that start a circle?" asked the woman.

Lamplighter recognized the woman as the chief financial officer of the hospital. He also knew her from her position as assistant track coach at the local Christian school as she was the subject of several of his interviews.

"Well, the Salvation Army uses that money to pay me to stand here," added Lamplighter.

"OK, but how does that relate to me?" questioned the woman.

"I then use that money to pay my monthly payments at the hospital," said Lamplighter. "The hospital then uses that money to pay you."

"OK, so you obviously know me," stated the woman. "But - um .. who are you?"

Lamplighter looked up and removed his scarf.

The woman laughed "Don Lamplighter, long time no see."

There was a three-second pause in the conversation as neither Lamplighter nor the woman had anything else to say.

"So what medical bill are you paying?" asked the woman.

"I'm still paying off the emergency room bill from when I gashed my arm trying to rescue that baby from the car accident in June," replied Lamplighter.

"Don't you have insurance?" she asked.

"Not since I got laid off from the paper," he replied. "I can't afford that, rent, food and car payments, so we just pay the Obamacare fine."

"So you are paying off a bill from injury you got for rescuing somebody else," said the coach while tilting her head to the side.

"That about sums it up," Lamplighter said as he shrugged his shoulders.

"Well, maybe I can do something about that," noted the woman just before walking into the store. "Merry Christmas"

"Merry Christmas to you as well," replied Lamplighter with a top of his hat.

Lamplighter was dressed for the warm weather. He wore the same clothes he had on the day before, except for a change of T-shirt socks, underwear, and the scarf.

The temperature had dropped another 10 degrees to an even zero.

His shift today was the same as Monday, 9 a.m. to 3 p.m. Lamplighter was just 30 minutes into his day, so he decided to start his singing. He got through one chorus of "Silent Night" when the woman walked back out of the store. She looked at Lamplighter and just shook her head. Lamplighter responded with a huge grin before singing the rest of the lyrics.

The song reminded him of his morning Bible study, which continued on the topic of Christmas. He took Captain Irving's suggestion and read Isaiah, which explained that Christ would be born unto the descendants of David.

He got through "Rudolph the Red Nosed Reindeer" and started "Let it Snow," when an older woman stood next to him and clapped along before making a donation.

The two traded Christmas greetings as she went into the store.

The rest of the hour followed a similar pattern with singing, donations and good clean holiday fun.

Around 10:30 a.m., he had another visit from a familiar face, Happy Evans, a former colleague.

"Yo, Hap," yelled Lamplighter. Evans said nothing, but immediately turned to Lamplighter as the two shared a hearty handshake.

"What brings you out in the cold?" inquired Evans.

"Earning money to pay the bills and get Gloria a little something for Christmas," replied Lamplighter.

Lamplighter and Evans were former co-workers at the local daily newspaper. They got along well there - to the point that they volunteered to ring together three years ago.

"I ask the same question of you," said Lamplighter.

"I have to get my medicine," said Evans shaking his head.

Evans is now 58 years old and has had many health problems. He told all of them to Lamplighter during the three years that they worked together.

Evans donated a buck to the kettle.

"I had a tumor removed from my arm," Evans continued. "I've been prescribed some vitamins and other supplements to take during my chemo."

"Pretty good idea," noted Lamplighter. "My mom and dad both had cancer. They both said that going through the treatment can be harder than going through the disease itself."

"I heard that as well," said Evans. "I think the vitamins will help."

Lamplighter started singing again as a black limo pulled up. He could not see the license plate which made him wonder if it was part of Absalom's fleet, as the only person to come out of the car was a short middle aged man.

The man passed Evans in the enclosed door area of the drug store.

Lamplighter and Evans waved to each other. Lamplighter started singing. He got through "Sleigh Ride," "White Christmas," and "Jingle Bells" before the man returned to the limo.

Lamplighter did not recognize the man, but he was able to get a good look at the plates - fork - a chess term with which he was familiar. It was definitely one of Absalom's collection. It left Lamplighter's mind racing as to what they were doing in Canandaigua.

He didn't have time to think about the situation as Sheriff J.P. Cornell pulled up to the store to talk with Lamplighter.

"I want to say I'm sorry that one of my deputies pulled you over last night," said Sheriff Cornell.

"I appreciate the apology, but I assure you that it is not necessary," replied Lamplighter. "I understand that they are just doing their job."

"Do you know why they pulled you over?" asked Cornell.

"Yes but I want to hear you explain it again," said Lamplighter, who took the recorder out of his pocket.

Sheriff Cornell laughed and started his comment.

"It is your car and license plate," answered Cornell. "Remember the guy who attacked you here yesterday?"

"How could I forget," remarked Lamplighter.

"Well not only does he drive the same little black Neon as you, but he also has the same three

Letters on his plates - DML," explained Cornell.

"So .... Am I going to get pulled over everywhere I go?" questioned Lamplighter.

"I made sure that every law enforcement unit in the county has the plate number," said Cornell.

"You shouldn't be bothered, but I apologize in advance if you are.

"Well, then Merry Christmas, but I am curious as to how you knew I was here," stated Lamplighter.

"I went to your house first and your wife told me," answered Cornell. "Merry Christmas to you"

Cornell left, but as he went through the exit, he was passed by Gloria, who had arrived for Lamplighter's lunch.

"Ironic," said Lamplighter as he opened the door and placed the kettle on the floor in the front seat. "Sheriff Cornell and I were just talking about you."

"Yeah," replied Gloria. "I just told him where you were."

Don took a restroom break inside the store and picked up a copy of the Canandaigua paper on his way out. He returned to the car to a refill of hot coffee and a surprise treat - two hot homemade turkey melts. Gloria smiled as she showed off a small cup of milk.

"Thanks," said Lamplighter just before saying a prayer asking for a blessing for the meal.

Gloria has also made some ham melts for herself. Both of them chowed down not leaving much room for conversation.

"These hit the spot," grunted Lamplighter. "I love you, thanks."

"I love you too," said Gloria as she pulled out a bag of chocolate chip cookies.

The couple gobbled them down as well as Don soon had to get back to his bell.

"Happy Evans, a hospital administrator and a very happy fan of my singing," said Don.

"Too easy," replied Gloria. "Three people who donated at the bell this morning."

They kissed just before Lamplighter exited his car, making sure he had everything he needed.

Gloria drove off as Lamplighter set up the tripod.

The remaining hours of Lamplighter's shift was uneventful, featuring just music and donations. He took the time to perform his morning Wing Chun routine. He needed one more restroom break, which led to another session of playing with the toy car. The relative calmness allowed him to do a bit of wondering as to why Absalom was in Canandaigua, or if he was even in the limo at all.

Captain Irving arrived at 3 p.m. with a fresh bell ringer and to take Lamplighter to Gloria's store. As they exited the parking lot, they passed another black Neon. The plates were not even close to his. Lamplighter just laughed.

Chapter 11

Jacob Glass was laughing too.

Glass holds a full-time job working at Bob's, a popular deli in downtown Canandaigua. It is his first-ever job as well. Glass had a good laugh at the hands of the company's owner, Bob Brock. Brock, now 60 years old, was a local high school football star. He then went on to make a name for himself at both the college and professional level. He opened the restaurant 31 years ago after his playing days were over. He had hoped that it would stay in business based on his name alone, but he stayed in business due to a countywide reputation for having the best sandwiches.

Customers get both a good sandwich and a laugh from one of Bob's clean, funny jokes.

"What kind of dog do you use to wash your hair?" said Brock to his crew during a lull between the lunch crowd and the customers that came for the dinner hour.

None of his employees responded as Block took a slow look around the kitchen.

"A shampoodle," he yelled with a gleeful facial expression as he was scratching his nearly-bald head.

The irony of his lack of hair was enough to get his staff, including Glass, rolling with laughter.

Brock liked to listen to the radio in the kitchen. He had it turned to a station that was featuring a local news talk hour. The topics included Monday evening's robbery of the bell ringer at Clock grocery. Feeling nervous, Glass went outside for his break. It was cold and he was not properly dressed for the occasion, but he needed the smoke to help stave off his drug cravings during his work shift.

Brock was especially interested in the story since he is a member of the Salvation Army band, which is where he met Lamplighter. Brock plays the tuba, while Lamplighter plays the trumpet. Both of them are devout Christians, but not official members of that church.

Despite that, Lamplighter had only been in the restaurant twice. Once when a captain had taken him there as a thank you for helping move some equipment. The second time was with Happy Evans, who bought sandwiches for both him and Gloria as a thank you for all of his training at work. Lamplighter likes the food, but is not able to afford to visit restaurants that often due to his limited budget.

Glass is at the place Tuesday through Friday from 9 a.m. until 5 p.m. and one day per weekend. He got his job at the restaurant because of Brock's good nature and desire to help out society by giving others a second chance. Glass is a high school drop-out who has spent two short stints in jail. He is currently on probation. One of the county probation officers put Glass in touch with Brock to get the job.

Glass comes in early for the purpose of cleaning the restaurant to get ready for its 11 a.m. opening. Once Bob's opens, Glass serves to clean up the plastic baskets after each customer visit. He uses the time between the crowd rushes to give the store another cleaning before helping out in the dining area again until leaving at five.

Once Glass left the restaurant, he almost instantly sought another hit of meth. He helps this by smoking cigarettes. His favorite place to get them is at a drug store downtown, the same store where he had attacked Lamplighter just the previous morning.

Upon entering the store, Glass estimated that the ringer at this kettle was 70 years old and alone. He also noted that there was a parking spot right behind her. Glass formulated his plan while waiting in line for his smokes. He decided that he would go straight to his car, park behind her leaving it running. He would then make sure that he was wearing his green gloves and strike her in the head. That should knock her out leaving an unguarded bell and a very easy getaway.

All that he needed to do was check for cameras on his way out. Seeing none, he put his plan into action. It was even easier then he thought. He punched the elderly lady just three seconds after getting out of the car. One second later the kettle was off of the tripod. He had left his door open and was back in his car and driving off three seconds later. There were no witnesses.

"Well that was easy," Glass thought to himself.

Glass changed his M.O. by keeping a pair of bolt cutters in his car. He parked in the abandoned industrial park on the northwest side to cut the lock and remove the cash, Not wanting to get caught with any evidence, he drove to Sonnenberg Park on the northwest side of the city and left the kettle in some bushes. Since he kept his gloves on, there were no fingerprints on the red money holder. He then went to meet his favorite drug dealer at Baker Park on the southwest edge of Canandaigua to get his fix.

Glass counted his money once he returned to his apartment. He had $35 in cash left over from the night's events. It was his second successful heist. The high he got from the thrill of the theft was just as good to him as the one he got from taking the meth he purchased from the proceeds of his crime.

He took the drugs anyway and began stomping around his apartment. Glass tired himself out and sat on the couch to dream of his next target.

Chapter 12

Lamplighter was planning as well. His goal was to avoid working on Christmas Eve.

The majority of his journalism income is derived from assignments given to him by the Victor News. So far this week, he had two stories due - an extended version from Monday night's shooting at the town board, and Tuesday's night's town board meeting in Farmington.

The Farmington meeting was recently added to the News's coverage area in order to help increase circulation. It was a natural choice since it was nestled between Victor and Canandaigua. The decision worked for the News as the number of subscribers went up 40 percent since the decision was announced September 1.

Lamplighter appreciated the move. It gave him job security by adding an area through which he already traveled on other assignments. The extra night also came on Tuesdays, which was already his night off from Wal-Mart.

A wrench was thrown into the plans this week since his customary deadline day Sunday was also Christmas Day and therefore his last day to work on his stories - Saturday fell on Christmas Eve.

"Chestnuts roasting on an open fire," hummed Lamplighter as he went into the family's townhouse.

It was around 3:30 p.m. Lamplighter had just returned from getting the one working family car from Gloria's store. On a normal day, he would be practicing his kung fu right now, but since his goal was not to have to work on Christmas, he got busy writing the follow-up story from Monday night's attack. Part of his effort included watching the 24-hour local news channel for its version of the story. He listened to national radio news while working. The President of the

United States took advantage of the Victor shooting to give yet another speech pushing for gun control and encouraging people to vote for people who supported his plan.

"That is one reason why we have that collapsible Xpectre Rapture bow," thought Lamplighter as he looked down at what he and Gloria called their "Apocalypse Box."

"Oh the weather outside is frightful," Lamplighter started singing as he waited for his circa 2004 computer to wake up.

He also read the online version of Canandaigua's daily paper. It claimed that the Sheriff knew the name of the attacker, but did not release it in order to do more investigating. He got to work right after checking his email, deleting a five-item list of worthless sales offers. His first order of business was to translate the quotes. Once that was done, it was a simple matter of writing his notes, which was basically Lamplighter's version of the events that he quickly noted after the shooting. He also left a message for the Sheriff's office to get more details.

The process didn't take too much thought as far as writing, but did require quite a bit of typing. He finished at 5:45 p.m.

The time frame barely gave him enough time to take a brief shower, grab a quick snack and pour himself some iced coffee. He had made himself a batch the previous night in order to keep himself awake through the Victor meeting and thought ahead enough to have a serving remaining for Tuesday's assignment.

"Oh Holy Night," he said as he started to get dressed.

It is his favorite Christmas song even though he finds it the most difficult to sing.

A traditional check of his equipment and he was on his way out the door.

"Merry Christmas neighbor!" said Matt, who lives one door down as he was entering his home. "Dressed up again I see."

"Of course," said Lamplighter. "I have another board meeting to cover. Merry Christmas to you."

Lamplighter was wearing a long-sleeve white dress shirt with a novelty Christmas tie along with dress pants and casual shoes. The only items of his attire that indicated the cold temperature were his big blue jacket and a pair of gloves.

"As we continue the holiday season, it is important to remember the spiritual battle that is taking place," said radio host Dr. Joe Hammill as Lamplighter started the car.

He gave the car time to warm up, which gave him more time to listen to the show. On the discussion agenda was the poor economy and how it led to lower spending amounts during this Christmas season. Lamplighter recalled the past few months at Wal-Mart and nodded in agreement.

"People are doing it right by not spending on holiday presents and saving money for the poor economy, which people feel is getting worse," said the guest, a 40ish man whom Lamplighter has yet to identify.

Commercials came next, which prompted Lamplighter to hit the road for the meeting.

The road to Farmington starts out the same way as the route to Victor. Lamplighter almost takes the path without even thinking - left out of the lot, left at the end of the street, right on Main Street, then stay on that road until the edge of town.

Lamplighter spent the time listening to more economic analysis. The road to Farmington veers to the right at the city limit. Just then the conversation on the radio took a veer as well. A new guest spoke about the traditions of Christmas.

"Is there a war on Christmas? ... Absolutely," said the guest, who identified himself as a professor of history. "It's all part of the plan. Christianity is the only thing that is preventing them from carrying out a one-world, futuristic feudal system under the guise of either environmental regulations or whatever global crisis they can manufacture."

"And if they can turn one of our most important holidays into a secular event, then it becomes easier to make up lies to discredit the faith," added the host. "Remember Christianity is a reality, not a religion."

The comments were followed by more commercials, which allowed Lamplighter time to think about the meaning. That did not last for as long as he wanted.

The road to Farmington Town Hall is full of hills and curves that can make winter travel dangerous. It runs mostly through forests and farmland until reaching the park and suburban area of the town.

The Lamplighters have taken that road several times during summertime leisure excursions. It is usually fun to ride in the summer, but Lamplighter realized that Western New York state weather can change that in a hurry.

One of the curves that worried him proved that point. As Lamplighter successfully slowed enough to make it around, he spotted a vehicle that came from the other direction that obviously did not. An elderly couple driving a small Volkswagen, a vehicle smaller than his, was stuck on the hill surrounding the road.

"Ugh, here we go again," Lamplighter thought.

After finding a safe place to park, he walked about 100 feet along the side of the road to find the car.

"Everyone OK in here?" he asked the male driver who had rolled down the window due to Lamplighter's request.

"Well, yeah," replied the female passenger, "except we're stuck."

Lamplighter took a walk around the car. It looked like it wasn't in deep. He thought he could push the car out himself. Since he would have to push it downhill, the physics would be on his side as well.

Lamplighter explained his idea to the couple, who graciously accepted his help. Being on the hill just off of the road, he had the advantage of looking on both sides of the road for a safe time to make his push. Two cars passed in each direction before he felt safe.

After giving a thumbs up, Lamplighter leaned against the hood of the car as the driver put the Volkswagen into reverse. Just as he predicted, Lamplighter was able to push the car down the hill and back into the road. Unfortunately, he did it so fast that he fell flat on his face on the hill and slid down into the ditch.

Covered in mud, he stood up to give a thumbs-up to the couple. They drove off as he hiked the short distance to his car.

"I guess I didn't learn my lesson from helping out that car stuck on the tracks," laughed Lamplighter as he took a short glance at his wounded left arm.

He brushed himself off before getting into the car and turning up the heat for the rest of the trip. He had about three miles to go before getting to the town hall. To brighten his mood, Lamplighter switched the station from Dr. Joe Hammill to Christmas music. He sang along to "Do You Hear What I Hear" and "Oh Come All Ye Faithful." He hummed along to an instrumental version of "Sleigh Ride" as he turned into the parking lot and stayed in the car to finish the tune and gather his materials for the meeting.

He took a quick glance around the lot and was in an even better mood.

"No limo," he gleefully mumbled to himself on the way to the door. "and no protesters."

Chapter 13

The limo was on the other side of the county.

Absalom and his crew with no name were back at their favorite hidden luxury resort just south of Canandaigua. The last time they were, the gathering ended with a sacrifice to their beloved Lucifer.

In the winter, the festival is for fun.

"I'm looking forward to this," Absalom said to his crew as he was overlooking the preparations.

He was recently promoted to state chairman of the secret society based on his computer skills and the prowess he showed in organizing the summer gathering. That fact gave him the authority to choose the location of the winter event. To him the location was obvious.

"Have a lot of good memories about this place?" he asked Julius while they were getting some logs together for a yule log ceremony.

"Many," was the reply. "But what are we doing with this Christmas tradition in our party?"

"Good question," replied Absalom. "I've researched this. The yule term is actually Anglo-Saxon and means both a feast and the alcohol that was consumed in tremendously large quantities at that time."

"Like we are going to do tomorrow night," noted Julius.

"Correct," laughed Absalom. "Isn't it amazing how far pagan rituals have infiltrated Christian traditions?"

"So there is a war on Christmas," added Julius with a nod. "And we are winning."

The location was ideal for this festival. He only expected about 75 patrons from across New York State to attend, leaving plenty of room in the ball room for the dinner-dance. The spot was also hidden from the public from any public roads, yet close enough to a state road that makes it easy for members of the group to arrive.

Absalom's favorite spot was the grand ballroom, which was where he and his crew were putting together the finishing touches for what they expect to be a raucous occasion.

He continued to supervise the preparations, approaching Gabrielle, who was decorating what she called a Solstice tree.

"I suppose you are going to tell me the real origin of this," she said with a grin.

"Of course, how else can I show off our organization's progress?" He said.

Absalom picked up some gold glass ornaments and started scouting the tree for an ideal location.

"This actually goes back to winter solstice celebrations quite far into history," explained

Absalom. "Even Druids have what they called a "holy oak.""

He then placed his selected ornament on the tree.

"So are you going to tell me why you picked the gold one?" inquired Gabrielle.

"I just like it because investing in it makes me, and therefore you and the rest of the organization a lot of money," he replied.

"You always think about money," Gabrielle said with a sigh.

"Of course," said Absalom as he picked up a wreath. "Besides green and gold are tied for my favorite color."

Absalom placed the wreath on the main door just as Madam Stephanie was coming into the building from having a cigarette. She had three women with her in order for Absalom to pick his date.

"Hey did you know that a wreath is actually an ancient Greek symbol for victory?" he asked as he selected his companion for the evening.

"We do now," said Alexander as he raised a glass of wine to the festival.

After making his selection he led her through the main arch in the ballroom. He stopped and kissed her under the mistletoe, then explained to her that it was actually a Norse pagan custom and that the early Christian church did not allow it in their building.

"I'm proud of all of you," said Absalom as he was still under the arch when Christianity first started its celebration of the nativity, it fell on the same day as the pagan holiday Brumalia and Christians were encouraged to celebrate as a way to take the holiday away."

Alexander gave him a glass of wine. All of the members of the group with no name raised a glass.

"We took it back from them," he cheered as they all raised a glass. "That means more profit for us."

Absalom then found a bowl, wrote the names of each of his trusted inner circle on a piece of paper and placed the pieces in the bowl. He then shook it and instructed his companion to pick out a name.

She reached in and silently handed the name to him.

"Steve," he said. "Congrats, you have to play the king of fools tomorrow. Think of someone you want to mock."

"I have it picked out already," replied Steve with a grin.

Chapter 14

Mud-soaked Don Lamplighter walked into the Farmington Town Hall meeting room without saying a word.

The room was the most basic of all of the three meeting areas that he covers. It reminded him of the fellowship center in his church back in Wisconsin, but half the size. On one side sits two folding tables connected to each other to make one big long space for the town council. One on end sits 50-year old farmer Al Messerman, around the corner and facing the audience is 45-year-old mechanic Kevin Garfield. Next comes the town supervisor - a retired banker named Dave

Adams. Town Clerk Peggy Ward starts the next table, followed on her left by John Sawyer, 43-year-old restaurant owner. The newest member of the board - a 28-year-old feed mill truck loader named Bill Jay - sits on the corner facing Messerman.

A table off the side contains Public Works Department Director Jeffery Craig, Water and Sewer Manager Tim Johnson and Code Enforcement Officer John Floyd. All three are approximately 50 years old and have at least 20 years of experience at their jobs.

All nine chuckled as Lamplighter walked into the room.

"OK, what happened to you?" asked Adams.

"You know same old," started Lamplighter. "Pushed car out of ditch ... went too fast ... fell in the mud."

Everyone in the room laughed as Lamplighter made his way to a table in the back of the room and placed his notebook and camera on it. He took off his jacket, hung it on a chair and sat.

"Well, at least your shirt stayed clean," laughed Floyd.

The audience of about 20 people responded in kind.

The board began discussing the minutes from the meeting two weeks as Lamplighter surveyed the room.

It was a typical crowd for a Farmington meeting. The front row consisted of the town assessor, fire chief and the same elderly couple that sat in the same spot at every meeting since Lamplighter started the assignment. He counted 15 students who were there as a result of a class requirement and Randall Meyer with a briefcase. Farmington was not a member of GEI so Lamplighter was curious to see what he had to say.

As usual, none of the members of the council offered a debate since all five, and Adams, were members of the same political party.

Meyer gave a two-minute presentation on GEI. He started by noting that Victor had joined the group and Canandaigua was considering it. Meyer continued to explain the importance of sustainability. He closed by handing out brochures.

"This is about the future," he said in closing. "We need to leave a clean planet for our children."

Meyer gathered his belongings and left the room after his time. Lamplighter followed him out.

"May I please have one of those brochures?" asked Lamplighter.

"Oh hey," replied Meyer as he gleefully handed over the information. "Don Lamplighter from the Victor News."

"Thanks for recognizing me," replied Lamplighter. "Do you have a few minutes to talk?" "A few, what do you need to know?" offered Meyer as they sat on a bench in the lobby.

"You seem to be doing a push to get GEI involved in the area, why is that?" asked Lamplighter. Meyer explained that he grew up in the area when it was known for heavy industry. Since then, people have been moving out to the Rochester suburbs, specifically mentioning Victor and Farmington as townships that had growing populations.

"It is important for the future that we develop the area correctly," he added.

"I have to ask this as a reporter," noted Lamplighter. "But who is to say what is correct?"

"Our kids and the Earth will tell us that," Meyer replied as he leaned back in a standoffish manner. "If 30 years from now this area is an environmental cesspool, we have nobody to blame but ourselves."

"OK," continued Lamplighter. "How did you get involved?"

Meyer told the story of how he moved to Victor to escape Rochester, which he called a "polluted city" and wanted to help. When he heard about the "Green Team" from his neighbor, he had to get involved.

"They elected me president," he said. "I did my due diligence by looking for a larger organization to help us. When I found GEI on the web, I liked what I saw."

Lamplighter told the story of how he heard Dr. Joe Hammill and his guest talk about GEI. And how some towns are seeing protest directed at the group.

"Those people are just telling lies because they don't care about the environment," responded Meyer. "I have four children and I want the planet to be healthy for them."

Meyer stormed off. Lamplighter just shrugged his shoulders and walked back into the room just as Johnson was talking about an inquiry he received from a person who owns a campground and wants to hook up to the sewer system.

The agenda featured nine resolutions, none of which were about the same topic. The council passed each one 5-0.

Lamplighter decided to use the campground inquiry as the lead and interviewed Johnson to get some details.

"If the campground expands, it can bring tourists into the area," interrupted Adams. "It can be another way to grow the economy of Farmington."

Lamplighter collected his equipment.

"At least nobody got shot tonight," he mumbled as he donned his jacket and left the room.

He then met with Steve Clive at Dunkin Donuts.

Clive gave him a history of his organization, which calls itself "Citizens Against The Tax" and handed Lamplighter a brochure. Clive explained that the group was started as soon as the tax was passed by the council two years ago. He did note that only two members of the current council - Cavanaugh and Cooper - were on the council at that time.

"I'm dumbfounded," he said. "We are telling the truth, but nobody is listening."

"I am going to tell you who the shooter is too," he added. "He is Roger Shawn."

Clive described Shawn as a military veteran who moved into Victor three months ago after taking a job at the Mall. He has been part of the group for about two months.

"I talked with every one of the Citizens," Clive added. "Nobody claimed to know what Shawn had planned. Another thing, I am sickened that the president is using this to push for more gun control."

The two exchanged business cards before Lamplighter headed home.

"I will keep in touch if I have any more questions," he added.

Clive just nodded as they shook hands.

Lamplighter listened to Christmas music on the way home. He arrived at his townhouse at 9 p.m.

There was another telephone message from his dad. He finally was able to change his pants, shoes and socks before picking up Gloria.

Snow started falling as he left to pick up Gloria. The both commented on its beauty during the drive back to the town house. Don quickly wrote up his notes on the Farmington meeting. He then translated the quotes from the meeting.

He took a break as the couple shared a frozen pizza while watching a DVD of Christmas cartoons. In adherence to his goal of getting his stories done before the holiday festivities, he finished that night's meeting story by 2 a.m.

Gloria stayed up to work on a Christmas project that she was giving to their friends. They did their random Bible study by reading the first chapter of Philippians. And found them encouraging. Given his battles with his new enemies, Don was especially strengthened by Verse 28 "And not in any way terrified by your adversaries, which to them is a proof of perdition but to you of salvation and that from God." They went to bed together for several games of triples.

Chapter 15

A winter morning added another step to Don Lamplighter's morning ritual.

His morning devotional was Micah 5:2 which told that the ruler would be born in Bethlehem

"But thou Bethlehem Ephrata, though thou be little among the thousands of Judah yet out of thee shall be come forth unto me that is to be ruler in Israel whose goings forth have been from of old, from everything.

Lamplighter started humming "O little Town Of Bethlehem" as he took a look out his bedroom window to ask a simple question - do I have to shovel this morning?

"I guess yes," said Lamplighter with a grin as he peeked out the curtain on Wednesday.

Not only did he have to shovel out his car, but he also had a double task - that of shoveling out the entrance to the townhouse parking lot.

"I'm going to love this," he thought to himself with a grin as he started putting on his warm winter gear.

He wore the same garb for shoveling as he did for bell ringing. He put on his two pairs of socks, underwear, long-sleeve shirt, polo shirt with a long tail and jeans in the bedroom. His dressing woke Gloria. She rolled over to look at the alarm clock. It was 11:11 a.m., just four minutes before the clock was set to deliver its shout.

"Let me guess," she said as she turned to look at Don. "Snow shoveling time"

"Oh you bet," replied Don, still with a grin. "You know how much I love to do this."

"Just don't hurt your bad leg," added Gloria. "You still have to work you know."

"True," replied Don. "But I fear that if I don't go and shovel right now, our poor little Neon won't make it out of the lot."

"City trap us in again?" said Gloria, as she sat on the side of the bed. "You know they always do," stated Don as walked out of the room, rolling his eyes.

His experience living in cold climates has taught him to watch out for that eventuality every time he shovels out a driveway. The community will invariably plow the entrance back up. The end effects are that both the street and the parking area are clear and the car is cleaned up, but a big pile of snow is pushed across the entrances. Removal of that snow is required before one can go anywhere. Even though he loves to shovel, he does get frustrated at having to free the same area twice. This was not the case today. He did have two areas to clear, but both places could be one-and-done.

"I hope they don't come by again," Don thought to himself.

Don took in the weather report on TV as he put on his boots. It was warmer today - 25 degrees - with a barely measurable wind speed of 3 mph.

Gloria arrived downstairs as Don was putting on his jacket. She was quickly followed by the cat, which took off for the kitchen right away, expecting her breakfast.

"How about a nice egg sandwich and hot cocoa when you come in?" offered Gloria.

"Sounds great," said. Don as he grabbed the shovel, which the Lamplighters placed on a tile part of the living room, right next to the door. "I look forward to it."

Lamplighter shut the door and looked down to find that the snow on the walkway was about two inches deep.

"It looks like I have a third place to shovel," he said to himself.

He made it through the pathway that leads to his door by pushing the shovel in front of him and struggling to control it with his left hand as he walked with his cane in his right.

Lamplighter took a left turn to get down the two steps that led to the main sidewalk and eventually the parking lot.

"Whew," he said with a deep exhale as he reached the lot and turned around to view his handiwork. "Safer for Gloria .... and Matt."

Lamplighter reached his Neon, which sat cold two spaces down on the left. The plow company contracted for the parking lot clears the spaces that are empty by piling the snow around any car that is left. Since the Lamplighters typically don't leave until late morning or early afternoon, they almost always fall victim to this technique.

The snow was high enough this morning that all four tires and both license plates were covered.

"I'll get you soon, good girl," he said as he patted the Neon on the trunk in a similar fashion to the way he pets his cat.

The only other car that was covered was the Lamplighter's gold Dodge Stratus, was four spaces down. Snow was piled higher around this vehicle since it was not in working order and fell victim to the plow company on every visit.

"You too," he said after clearing away a spot on the trunk to pat it. "Once I can make enough money to fix you up."

He continued past seven more spaces before reaching the entrance to the lot. The first thing Lamplighter did was shove his cane into a snowbank on his left. This had a dual purpose - placing the cane out of his way and marking the edge of his expected shoveling area.

Plows have formed the snow into a barrier that Lamplighter estimated to be eight inches high and one-foot wide. It was an obstacle that would be difficult for the old Neon to transverse, but relatively easy for him to eliminate.

"I love this," said Lamplighter as he got to work.

With each pass of his shovel, he was able to clear a small area straight through to the street. Lamplighter put the full loads on the bank closest to him. In just ten loads, he had cleared a path big enough for one car.

Taking advantage of the situation was Matt, who was coming home for lunch.

"Thanks," she said as she stopped on her way through. "This give you a lot of exercise I suppose?"

"It does and I have to go to work," replied Lamplighter.

"Well, Merry Christmas," she said as she drove away, not leaving time for Lamplighter to reply in kind.

Lamplighter hummed the songs that he will perform at the concert as he shoveled. He is part of two numbers. He is slated to join the band to play "Carol of the Bells" and sing in the grand finale choir number "Oh Come All Ye Faithful."

The bus pulled up just as he was finishing the last of what he counted to be 23 shovels full. "Have your Christmas shopping done yet?" said Mitch the bus driver through his window during his scheduled stop.

Lamplighter put his arms out wide.

"This is my gift to my fellow tenants," replied Lamplighter. The two had developed a professional-friendly relationship during the summer that Mitch spent working at Wal-Mart. They see each other often as Lamplighter frequently must take his bus to work.

"Yep that's the Don Lamplighter that I know," replied Mitch. "Merry Christmas to you and your wife."

This time Lamplighter had time to reply.

"To you and yours as well," he said.

Lamplighter grabbed his cane from the snowbank for the trek back to the Neon. His walking aid was placed on the roof of the Stratus for the purpose of getting it out of the way of his task. His plan was to start at the back of the car and progress down each side, dropping each load into the small area that passes for a front lawn of the nearest townhome.

Lamplighter noticed a Canandaigua police cruiser enter the lot, but took no mind to it and continued to clear off the Neon. He also worked from the top down, which left the license plate last. He was still humming his songs when he suddenly stopped.

"City police stop right there," came a loud shout from a yet unidentified voice from behind him.

Lamplighter decided to obey the commands and dropped the shovel. "Put your hands on the car," was the next command.

Lamplighter complied. The officer approached him and placed a handcuff on Lamplighter's right hand.

"Place your hands behind your back," said the officer, who then captured Lamplighter's other hand in the cuffs.

"Stay right where you are," said the officer as he got back in his car, leaving Lamplighter wondering what this was all regarding.

His answer came to him as he caught a reflection of himself in the window of the Neon.

"This again," laughed Lamplighter as the officer returned and released him.

"Sorry about that Mr. Lamplighter," said the officer. "I'm new in town and I didn't recognize you."

"Let me guess," he replied. "Somebody called in that they saw a Neon in the parking lot and think I'm the guy that attacked the Salvation Army bell ringers ... including myself."

"Once again, I apologize," said the officer, who never gave his name.

"Understandable, Merry Christmas," replied Lamplighter.

Lamplighter finished freeing his vehicle as the officer drove away.

"That might get annoying," he thought to himself.

As promised, Gloria had both an egg sandwich and cocoa ready for her husband. Don removed his jacket and boots as he sat down for breakfast just in time to get a frantic phone call from Steve Clive.

"It wasn't us," Clive shouted. "I swear it wasn't us."

"What wasn't you?" questioned Don.

"The rock throwing," Clive responded. "It wasn't us. I swear it wasn't us."

It was now 12:30 p.m. and time for the couple to get their news from the 24-hour channel.

The top story was from Victor. Nearly every window was broken in the village's downtown area. Witnesses claim that it was members of the group Citizens Against The Tax. The newscaster reminded the audience that the alleged assailant from Monday's Victor Town board meeting was also a member of the group.

"It looks like I have a fact-finding mission ahead of me," Don said to Gloria

Last night's antics of Jacob Glass was the second story, although the newscast still was not able to identify him by name.

"I'm actually hoping he comes after me on Friday so I can keep a hold of him next time," said Don after finishing a sip of cocoa.

"I want him to get caught before then," replied Gloria.

"Yeah, that would be better," added Don, who now took his last bite of the sandwich.

Don did his Wing Chun exercise and sat in his favorite chair. The snow shoveling adventure caused him to doze off in his favorite chair for a few minutes before getting ready for work.

Gloria looked over and smiled.

Chapter 16

"I'm ticked," said Professor Randall Meyer on the phone from his den.

"What? What?" was the initial reaction of the half-asleep 53-year-old man on the other end of the line. "Who? Who is this."

Meyer was still seething from the previous night's interview with Lamplighter.

"How dare he?" he asked as he was pacing around his den.

Meyer is a professor at the Genesee River Institute Technology, also known as G.R.IT. The university is known as one of the most technologically advanced in the country. He is the chair of the Environmental Science Department. Meyer holds a Bachelor of Science in both Botany and Geology from an equally prestigious college across town.

His academic success and research projects in climate study earned him a Rhodes' Scholarship to Oxford where he earned a Master of Science in Geology. Upon his return to the United States, he accepted a position teaching high school Earth Science at Victor Central School, where he now resides. Meyer also took to writing papers on Geology.

Meyer later was granted a doctorate from Cornell University, also with a field of study of geology. He parlayed that degree with his teaching experience to get hired as a professor at G.R.I.T. After eight years, he was named an Associate Chair of the Geology Department.

Following a United Nations study that he thought proved the existence of global warming, Meyer convinced the board at his school to form a new department to fight what he convinced them to be humanity's greatest threat.

"That guy is just a stupid reporter from an insignificant worthless weekly rag," said the still pacing Meyer. "How dare someone that dumb challenge how important our organization is. We are the last line of defense for the earth."

"Dr. Meyer?" said the voice on the other end of the line. "Is that you?"

Finally waking up was Charles Isadore. Isadore is the current President of GEI. He is groggy after spending the night with his girlfriend at a pre Winter Solstice party.

"Now what are you trying to tell me?" asked Isadore.

Isadore was responding from the mansion that he and his girlfriend share outside of Toronto, which is also the headquarters of GEI.

"I was asked some very inappropriate questions about GEI by some dumb reporter who probably has an IQ of 12," replied Meyer.

"OK what questions?" asked Isadore.

Isadore and Meyer have known each other since their time taking classes together at Oxford. Isadore studied Biology, but since they had a common interest in the environment, they were both part of the same clubs and social activities. Upon completing his education, Isadore decided to stay in Great Britain and joined a group of environmental activists. The group attended a United Nations climate summit in Brazil. It was there they joined with a team of scientists to form GEI. The stated purpose was to promote environmental awareness and serve as an advisory group to local communities that were seeking ideas on sustainable development.

Meyer gave background on his Monday night meeting in Victor and previous night's council session in Farmington. He has yet to mention Lamplighter's name, since he does not even remember it without looking at a business card.

"He asked me about protests across the country," continued Meyer as his wife brought in some coffee. "People claim that we are just an organization of control freaks who are setting up a secret global takeover."

"Oh, those crazy conspiracy theorists," replied Isadore. "These are the same people that still believe that the world is flat and that cigarette smoking doesn't cause cancer."

"Hey," said Isadore's girlfriend.

Isadore turned to his lover and placed his index finger to his lips to try to keep him quiet for the phone call.

Meyer took a sip of coffee, set the cup back down and began pacing the room again. He had planned to call from the office, but last night's snowstorm forced him to make the call from home.

"I know anyone who is intelligent enough to read should be able to tell that global warming is real," added Meyer.

"Just curious," asked Isadore. "Exactly what questions did he ask you?"

"Nothing specific," replied Meyer, who was still pacing. "He just asked if I knew about the protests in other cities and how I responded to them."

Isadore leaned back in his recliner.

"And you said what?' he asked.

"I just said that those people obviously just don't care about the environment," answered Meyer, who then explained that he walked away from the interview. "What do I do?"

"Exactly what you did. It is No. 5 in the rules for radicals - ridicule is man's most potent weapon," said Isadore. "We have used it so well that nobody believes these nut jobs that talk about global

108

conspiracies anyway. By the way, the cigarette and flat Earth lines are good to use too."

'That's all I have to do?" asked Meyer.

"Just keep talking about how important the environment is," added Isadore. "Keep talking about the importance of sustainability. You are smart, you will do fine."

"Thanks," responded Meyer.

"By the way," Isadore wondered aloud. "Who is the reporter?"

"Don Lamplighter," replied Meyer looking down at the business card the reporter had given him. Isadore hung up. Meyer sat down. The call to his friend had calmed him down giving him confidence to handle Lamplighter. It did however anger Isadore's girlfriend.

"Why did you shush me?" she asked while stomping the floor.

"He doesn't know about what GEI really does," said Isadore. "He is someone from Oxford who thinks that he is my friend."

"You seem to have a lot of those," said the lover.

"That is the point," said Isadore as he folded his hand in a fashion similar to Absalom. "We have more than 5,000 cities around the world giving us $7,200 a year. That is more than $5 million, not including private and corporate donations from those who know our real cause."

Isadore took a brochure off a desk and tossed it on the floor.

"All we have to do is hand out some brochures to our so-called friends and they convince people in all of these cities to implement our control grid," he continued to explain. "The best part of it is that they don't even know what they are doing for us."

The girlfriend picked up the brochure and placed it back on the desk.

"All we have to do is put out silly colored paper like this and we can convince people to live in ever shrinking apartments and give up driving cars," added the lover. "While we fly around in private jets and live in mansions. It's great.

Chapter 17

As Gloria dropped him off for work, Don Lamplighter noticed that nobody was paying attention to the bell ringer outside of the middle door at Wal-Mart. He went over to change that.

"You've got to live it up a bit," he said to the woman. "How about a song?"

Lamplighter sings for the customers as a way to lift the spirits of both himself and others during his shifts at the red kettle. Starting this holiday season, he began to surprise other ringers with the same tactic.

"How about "Rudolph the Red Nosed Reindeer" she asked.

The woman, who appeared to Lamplighter to be the same age as him, gave him her bell. She was with a teenage girl who Lamplighter assumed to be her daughter. The daughter cowered in the corner in embarrassment as the pair sang.

A crowd gathered to listen and started to put coins in the donation bucket. The group included children who joined in with responsive phrases. He kept singing his part, even though he couldn't really understand the replies except for "like a light bulb."

The crowd applauded. An elderly woman limped her way through to put a dollar in the kettle and requested "White Christmas."

Lamplighter looked at his watch he had five minutes before he needed to punch in for his shift at what is known as the seasonal department during the holidays, so he complied with a short verse. He lost his accompaniment as the woman who was working her ringing shift decided to just sit back and listen, as did the crowd of about 20 who stopped either on their way into or out of the store.

'Thanks I needed that," whispered the elderly woman as she gave him a big hug after the song.

Lamplighter replied "Merry Christmas."

He waved to the crowd as he went into the store. All employees were required to enter and leave for their shifts through this door. It happened to funnel him past the greeter who shook his head.

"So who was that you were singing with?" he asked.

"I have no clue," he replied. "I just felt like singing."

Lamplighter was in a rush to get to the time clock. He was scheduled to start at 2 p.m. It was now 2:01, but store policy allows for a five-minute grace period, leaving Lamplighter enough time to put his lunch in the fridge and get to the clock, he slid his card through at 2:04.

"Just in time," said Regis, the department manager. Regis was just finishing his break and happened to be at the clock.

"Yeah, just in time for our daily walk where you tell me the plans," replied Lamplighter.

Lamplighter went to get a walkie-talkie hooked it to his belt and put in his earpiece before the two hit the sales floor.

Regis didn't have assignments in particular. They talked about how it was now Wednesday and since Christmas was Sunday, it was expected that Lamplighter, and the rest of the night crew, would spend the night running registers for customers making last-minute purchases.

Regis pointed to an aisle that was previously stocked with Christmas items.

"Try to condense this area down after closing," he said. "We are going to use it for a discount section again."

"I call that the aisle of misfit toys," replied Lamplighter.

Regis got stopped to help a customer find a particular brand of dog food. Lamplighter continued to the garden registers. Only two checkout lanes were operating, each with seven customers.

Lamplighter opened up a third line. He didn't leave that post until two hours later for his break, which finally allowed him to check his cell phone. The phone buzzed to indicate an awaiting message. Lamplighter thought it would be Gloria with another round of triples, but instead it was

Professor Randall Meyer.

"I would like a word with you," said the message in a stern, but polite tone. "I need to talk a little bit more about GEI."

Lamplighter tried to return the call, but only got an answering machine.

"Hi, this is Don Lamplighter from the Victor News, I'm going to be unavailable for the rest of the night, but I can call you in the morning. You can call me back at this number. I look forward to talking with you."

Lamplighter sat by himself at one of the eight round tables that comprised the seating area of the Wal-Mart break room. Several employees were moving in and out of the room for the entire 15 minutes, but none of them sat next to him. He kind of liked it that way. It gave him time to read the daily newspaper from Rochester. The front-page story said that Roger Shawn was indeed the alleged assailant in Victor and that law enforcement had executed a search warrant of his apartment in Victor and found evidence that connected him to what they called "right-wing hate groups.".

"I can see where this is going," he sighed. "But, I wonder what happened to the donation kettle bandit."

He continued his search of the paper and was depressed at how both the national and world news painted a bleak picture of the near future. After that break, Lamplighter returned to the register for another two-hour stretch of continuous, yet uneventful customer contact. He was actually getting bored until a customer came through with an entire cartful of candy.

He recognized the customer as the coach and hospital executive from earlier this week.

"I work at the hospital and YMCA," said the coach. "I can stock up, because I'm expecting a lot of kids at both office parties."

"Glad we could help," responded Lamplighter, who was not really paying attention, his mind otherwise occupied by the message about GEI.

"I think I'm helping you," remarked the coach as she searched her wallet for a debit card. "What would happen to all of this candy otherwise?"

"I think they take it back," started Lamplighter. "Melt it back down and use it again for Easter stuff."

"That's funny," said the coach. "Merry Christmas"

"Same to you," he replied, still distracted by the cell phone message and harried by the continuous flow of holiday shoppers.

"That is the tastiest of all of the conspiracy theories," said the next customer.

Lamplighter just stared at him in the way one would when hearing a bad pun.

"Actually, I needed that," said Lamplighter after a short pause. "Merry Christmas"

Just like the first two hours of his shift, Lamplighter stayed on register for the duration until his lunch break. He punched out and, recognizing that he needed a quick mood boost, he went and sang with the bell ringer.

Lamplighter drew a crowd with his rendition of "Jingle Bells." The crowd responded with delight as he placed his hand on his ear to get a "ha-ha-ha" after singing the lyrics "laughing all the way."

He was having so much fun that he did not notice the black Neon drive by.

Lamplighter closed his improvised two-song set with "Sleigh Ride." The songs gave him the boost that he needed. Once back in the lunch area, he checked his phone messages. One was a text from Gloria ... a simple "MWA". The second was a voice response from Randall Meyer.

'Thank you for returning my call. I would appreciate the chance to respond to your questions from Tuesday night," said Meyer. "I can talk around 11 a.m."

Lamplighter caught the 24-hour news channel report on Shawn and the only thing new was a photograph. This was not new information to him since he actually witnessed the shooting. What concerned him just as much were shootings over the rest of the country. According to the news, the month of November had set a record for the country and December was on its way to breaking that mark. Politicians were lining up on both sides of the gun-control debate.

Lamplighter spent the rest of the lunch break wondering what Meyer was going to say. It put him in a bad mood.

Chapter 18

The Holiday season was just as busy at Bob's sandwich shop.

Jacob Glass needed the extra money, so he took Bob up on his offer to work an extra hour. This helped him out with his bills, but unfortunately for the rest of the Canandaigua, it placed Glass in a time crunch. His Monday surveillance put the bell ringing time over at approximately 6:30 p.m. Glass didn't get out his job until six p.m. He got in and out of the restroom and into his black Neon to find his next victim.

"This is going to be close," he thought to himself as he put a Death Metal CD into his car stereo.

He did a quick check of his equipment - a check that sounded just like Lamplighter collecting his reporter's equipment. Glass had put all of it in a bag then put that bag under the passenger seat.

After retrieving and unzipping it, he reviewed the contents - pepper spray, check; green gloves with tacks, check; big wooden stick, check. It was the exact same as he packed it earlier that day before he left for his job.

"All here," he thought to himself. "Now I just need a place to go."

The first place he tried was outside of the local independent grocery store. The place was only three blocks away from Bob's sandwich shop. By the time Glass got there, Salvation Army Lieutenant Mike Winters was there taking the kettle and bell from the ringer.

Glass left as soon as he saw them.

"Not the place," he thought to himself as he quickly drove away.

His next target was the drug store. It was six blocks away and across Main Street, but Glass figured that he could get there before Lieutenant Winters. He did, but given that Glass had already attacked the place twice, the Canandaigua Police Department made a point to watch the business.

"Shoot," Glass exclaimed as he pounded on his steering wheel.

Glass then surmised that it would take him too long to get to Victor for a visit to Clock Grocery.

"Well, this limits my options," he said to himself as he played the steering wheel like a set of drums.

Glass continued on the road toward Wal-Mart. He figured those would be the most profitable kettles and would therefore be the last two stations that would be closed for the evening. The route from the store to Wal-Mart was the same that the Lamplighters took to drop Don off for his shifts.

Glass reached the parking lot of Wal-Mart. He did a loop around so he would be facing the back exit by the bell ringers which would give him an easier getaway. Glass saw the first door, but was angered by the unusually large crowd that gathered around the kettle. A closer examination explained why - they were there to hear Lamplighter sing.

"I should have taken care of that guy Monday morning," he grunted as he again started to rapidly tap on his steering wheel.

He slowly drove toward the other kettle, only to see his best route to the kettle blocked by two Wal-Mart workers helping load some recent purchases into a minivan. Glass drove out of the lot empty-handed as his hands gripped the steering while he wondered what to do next.

"At least I could get my share of junk food," he thought to himself.

His preferred store to get his fix was Gloria's Dollar General store but he figured that he should not draw attention to himself and therefore chose his second option an overstock store in the strip mall across from Wal-Mart. The facility was largely abandoned save for three stores. One side was an auto repair store, which was right next to a furniture store. This left the mall with a large empty parking lot.

Glass made a beeline past those stores and the next four spots - all of which featured "For Rent" signs - until getting to his destination. He had a huge smile on his face as he got an unexpected surprise in a Salvation Army bell ringer and his traditional red tripod and kettle. Glass looked around for either a church van or police cruiser. Seeing none, he formulated a plan.

He counted eight cars in the lot and used them as a visual shield to hide his parking place from the ringer and any cameras. Glass left the Neon so that his car was facing out of the spot and he did not have to back up to get out.

Glass left the car running as he opened his container of pepper spray and donned his green gloves. The vehicle remained running as he put his hands in his pockets and walked toward the ringer. The man manning the kettle was a shade under six feet tall with a hefty girth. Glass was reminded of Lamplighter.

"This guy is about 20 years older, but it will be good practice for when I run into Lamplighter again," he thought to himself as he approached his target.

"Merry Christmas," said the gentleman.

Glass said nothing as he put two quarters into the pot, took his other hand out of his pocket and covered the man's face with pepper spray. He immediately followed by donning his green glove and connected with a right hook to the bell ringer's temple.

The ringer was staggered, but Glass felt that he needed the practice for another bout with

Lamplighter and followed with another right to the face and a kick to the right knee.

The ringer fell as Glass unhooked the kettle and ran back to his car.

"Good thing nobody comes here or I could have been spotted," he said as he drove off.

The only place in the area that was popular was a Taco Bell that was recently built in an outlying plot. The traffic from the restaurant worried Glass, so he made sure to drive carefully to avoid attention. It took him longer than he wanted, but he eventually got to his abandoned industrial area unscathed.

Glass cut off the lock and reached in, only to find $99.30.

"Maybe it isn't a good thing that people don't go to that store that much," he said.

Glass headed to the park across town to buy his hit for the night. He took a side trip to the deli and made it home for a fix of junk food.

Chapter 19

"That will be $102.90," said Lamplighter as he was back from lunch and at the register in the garden center of Wal-Mart.

"That is way too high you moron," replied the angry middle-aged woman. "I hate coming here because you people that work here are such idiots."

"Well, I still have time to change this," replied a discouraged Lamplighter. "Let's take a look at the receipt."

Lamplighter has been working at Wal-Mart for two years now and has made pretty much every mistake possible. He hated the fact that he has done that, but it did have the positive side effect of teaching him how to work his way out of any situation that arises at the register. Lamplighter hoped that this was one of those times.

"What good would that do with an idiot like you trying to solve the problem?" yelled the customer. "OK," said Lamplighter frankly. "Let's work on this together."

Lamplighter printed what he called "the slip," which is basically an unofficial version of the receipt that a cashier can use to review a transaction for any mistake. The irate customer grabbed the paper out of Lamplighter's hand. He printed another copy for himself and walked over to the customer's cart to count the items.

Lamplighter began to look through every bag and compared its contents to "the slip." He discovered an error in the sixth of 13 bags. There was only one green Christmas sweater while the slip said that there were two. Each sweater was $20. The exact amount that the customer thought the total was over her calculations.

Lamplighter fixed the problem by simply removing the extra item from the total. The register called for a manager; fortunately there was already one in the area. The transaction was easily approved with a turn of a key.

"Idiot," said the customer as she walked to the doors.

Lamplighter just shrugged his shoulders and took the next customer.

Commercialization of the holidays, have made it a pretty depressing time for Lamplighter to work at Wal-Mart. It was one of the things he appreciated the most about his time ringing bells, the idea that he could say "Merry Christmas" to each person that donated to the kettle.

Lamplighter had more on his mind. He was thinking about the person that was attacking bell ringers and what Professor Randall Meyer wanted.

The latter two thoughts were on his mind during his 9 p.m. break, The local news reported on the attack of the bell ringer and Lamplighter's cell phone contained a message from Professor Meyer.

"11 a.m. sounds good for me," said Meyer on the message. "Please call me on my home number 555-1029."

Lamplighter knew that he had a lot of research to do that night so he got himself a cup of coffee from the company-provided maker in the lunchroom. He took the last cup and helped out his fellow co-workers by brewing another full pot before sitting back down.

The last two hours of his shift were preoccupied with the same three topics – One, the holidays are too commercialized; Two, who keeps attacking bell ringers, and Three - what he was going to say about GEI in his conversation with Professor Meyer.

It was the first topic that took up the majority of space in his thoughts. His job over the last two hours was cleaning the garden center. He had fun decorating the place for the holiday season in early November, but found it depressing that it was now December 21 and nearly all of his efforts were taken down and sold to customers.

"All about money, nothing about Christ," he grumbled to himself as he swept the floors.

He started cleaning up the aisles and was able to condense half the merchandise down as requested by Regis. One of the ornaments he found had a musical motif. It reminded him that he had a concert coming up Saturday, so he did a mental rehearsal of his trumpet part in "Carol of the Bells" and his vocal part in "O Come All Ye Faithful." It boosted his spirits a little.

Lamplighter checked out for the night and found a message from his wife.

"Door," said the simple message from Gloria.

"On way," he replied.

"I've got a surprise for you," she said as Don got into the car.

"I hate surprises," replied Don.

"I know," continued Gloria, "but you will like this one, once I let you know, of course".

Don just sighed. Neither of them spoke until halfway home.

"What's on your mind?" asked Gloria.

"A guy I'm supposed to interview on the phone tomorrow, the guy who is attacking Salvation Army bell ringers and all of this stupid fake Christmas stuff at Wal-Mart," replied Don.

"Three things that are on your mind?" asked Gloria.

Don just looked at her in puzzlement. He then turned to look at her and grinned.

"That sounded like a triple didn't it?" asked Don.

"Is that a smile I see?" responded Gloria. "I didn't think you could do that anymore."

"It's in there sometimes," said Don, who couldn't think of anything better to say.

The two arrived home. Gloria asked Don to close his eyes as they entered the townhouse. Gloria had the day off and had decorated the living room in a Christian style for the holidays.

She had placed a Nativity on the book shelf, put up some lights all around the house and put up a small artificial tree that was decorated with ornaments of crosses, angels, churches and apples.

There was a small collection of presents under the tree.

"This actually is very pretty and I love the theme," Don said as they embraced in the middle of the room.

'Thanks," said Gloria as she looked up at him. "I can tell that you are not happy these days and I love you and wanted to do something special."

Don just hugged her in silence for five minutes.

"I love you, but I have to get up to work," said Don.

The Lamplighters then read their nightly Bible study, the third chapter of Hebrews, Verse 13 reminded Don of the role that Gloria took in the car. "But exhort one another daily while it is called today; lest any of you be hardened by the deceitfulness of sin." They kissed before Don headed for the computer room.

The story from the Farmington meeting was done, so he gave it a read and sent it to his editor.

He waited to talk to the Sheriff for the Victor meeting article. He then started his internet research of GEI.

His first stop was to GEI itself to get a bit of history. Nothing there gave him cause for alarm except for the fact that it had a lot of foreign influence. He then stopped at the sites from some of the groups that had protested the organization's action in their particular city. These stories were confirmed by a visit to Dr. Joe Hammill's site.

Lamplighter had never heard Gregg Matzek talk about the topic, but he decided to give his website a review anyway. A five-minute video made some startling claims. Lamplighter returned to the GEI site and printed out the official charter; it was exactly as Dr. Hammill said.

Lamplighter formulated the questions he was going to ask Professor Meyer.

Chapter 20

"Hello, welcome to the party," said Absalom to each guest that entered the great hall on the resort outside of Canandaigua.

He was proud of the job that he and his team had done decorating the facility for tonight's Winter Solstice party.

"A candy cane, are you kidding me?" scoffed the banker that arrived from Syracuse. "This is a party for adults."

He claims family lineage back to the clans of Europe. Because of that and his current profession, the banker expected to be named the chairman of the New York State branch of the global syndicate. A vote tally left him in second place with the main reason being Absalom's ability to make money for every member in the state.

"I'm well aware of the pagan origins of our society," he said as he looked down at Absalom.

This was easy to do with his 6-foot, 3-inch frame, compared to the 5-foot, 8 inch Absalom.

"I can see this party is going to be a waste of time and a bore for me," he continued with the same tone of disdain. "I would throw a much better party than this."

It was then that he received his escort for the evening, a petite redheaded woman wearing a long silver dress. The banker looked at her and smiled.

"Then again," he added. "It might be fun after all."

Absalom summoned Madam Stephanie to his side at the door.

"Great job," he whispered in her ear. "We are going to have plenty of blackmail material after tonight."

"Thank you," she added. "This is my specialty."

She then left to return to her charges. Absalom had given her an important job - research each guest and find the perfect companion to fit their taste. She had collected one for each guest, including herself and the rest of Absalom's captains. Her hires ranged from tall blond women to short fat men, depending on the preferences as discovered by Madam Stephanie.

The 75 guests included not only bankers, but each member of the global syndicate's strategically placed members. This group ranged from college professors to business people. It also included retired military personnel, politicians and influential members of the arts and entertainment industries.

Each guest took their seat with a prostitute in one hand and a candy cane on the other.

Absalom took the podium for his welcome speech.

"As all of you probably already know, I hate being in public, let along public speaking," he said to start his speech. "Well, not at much as Ken Knight at least."

His comment drew a small chuckle from the members of the society.

"I had decided to tell you how most of the alleged Christmas traditions that we are celebrating tonight have a root in pagan rituals, but all of you already know that as well," he continued.

Members of the society looked at each other and nodded in agreement.

"I actually find that part of the fun of celebrating like we do is that we have tricked Christians into using the same traditions," he stopped a moment to smile, "and we can have our celebrations right in their faces and they don't even know it."

Absalom then pulled out a Bible as the party guest recoiled in horror.

"I shall now read the sacred verses," he said before opening the Bible.

He first read Genesis Chapter 3, Verse 15 - "And I will put enmity between thee and the woman and between thy seed and her seed. It shall bruise thy head and though shalt bruise his heel."

The crowd hummed until Absalom read the second verse - John Chapter 8, Verse 44. - Ye are of your father the devil, and the lusts of your father ye will do. He was a murder from the beginning and abode not in the truth, because there is no truth in him. When he speaketh of his own for he is a liar and the father of it.

That verse was followed by Revelation Chapter 13, Verse 1. "And I stood upon the sand of the sea and saw a beast rise up out of the sea, having seven heads and ten horns and upon his horns, ten crowns and upon his heads the name of blasphemy."

A known Satan worshiping artist from New York City raised his glass. "Amen," he shouted.

"Keep that glass up there," said Absalom said, "For I am going to raise mine as well."

All of the party's attendees followed suit.

"Just think," continued Absalom. "In one year, we will have our man in the Oval Office and right after that, our chosen capital of the world."

The crowd stood up and cheered.

"So in the great Roman tradition, let's feast," he finished with his arms open wide.

Absalom took his seat. In order to help mingle, each one of his captains sat at a different table.

He sat with a politician, college professor and two stock brokers. Sitting next to him was his escort. Absalom was given an older woman of 5-foot-

11inches in height. She was wearing a gold dress, just the way he wanted. As per his request, she did not speak for the entire evening.

To make the evening even more special, Absalom placed Gabrielle, his top grifter, in charge of finding out what each guest would like for the festival meal. Absalom chose the stereotypical meal of one who spends most of his time on a computer - microwave TV dinner, a donut and an orange soda.

"Perfect, just what I wanted," he said to strange looks from both his guests and their escorts. His escort was given the same food that he had.

He returned to the podium after the meal.

"Wasn't that a great meal?" exclaimed Absalom to applause.

"Stand up Gabrielle," he said as the captain rose. "This is the lovely lady who made sure that each of you got the food of your desires."

The crowded applauded again.

"And now in the tradition of many cultures," he added as he waved his arm to acknowledge the adjoining dance floor, "let's dance."

He placed Julius in charge of selecting the music. Based on the results of a survey of the guests, he chose a mix of classical, jazz and big band. The one genre he avoided was traditional Christ- based Christmas carols.

Not one for dancing, Absalom just sat silent and motionless as he watched the frivolity from the side of the room. His prostitute complied and acted the same way. He did not speak until he felt a hand on his shoulder nearly two hours into the music.

"I was wrong," said the banker, who had his other hand on the small of his escort's back. "You put on a good show."

Absalom said nothing, only tapping the banker's hand and noticing his watch. It was 11 p.m.

'That reminds me," he said as he returned to the podium. "One more tradition to go - The king of fools."

On his cue Steve entered from a side room. He was wearing a fat suit, shirt and tie, fake glasses and was walking with a cane.

Absalom and the rest of his captains burst out laughing. "Don Lamplighter!" they said in unison.

Steve walked into the middle of the dance floor, yelled 'I'm a stupid Christian!" and fell on purpose.

All of Absalom's captains took a turn kicking him. The suit provided enough padding that Steve was not getting hurt from the blows. Absalom went last.

'That was certainly cathartic," he said to his escort as he sat back down next to her.

She just nodded.

The party continued until each guest adjourned themselves and their hired companion to their room for the night. Absalom sat silently reviewing the room, satisfied with a job well done. He got off of his chair and extended his hand to his guest. She held it as they left for his private suite in the guest wing of the resort.

Chapter 21

Steve Clive thought he had a great idea.

The concern among the Citizens Against The Tax is that they were not getting enough positive attention. Clive decided that despite the winter weather, a 24-hour vigil could at least draw some notice to the cause.

"This place is well lit." he said to three members of his group. "Plus there is a camera watching it."

It was 11 p.m. and the four were on the Donaldson's lawn. They lived on Main Street in Victor.

The group agreed that his residence was the ideal place to hold its event.

In addition to Donaldson, Clive was joined by Jill Ball, a 35-year-old unemployed accountant and Mary Hutch, a 48-year-old widow who was struggling to support her family after her husband died of cancer. All three of Clive's friends were homeowners and shared the same concern. They were visibly armed with guns.

"This tax is going to devastate us." said Ball. "Who the heck came up with the idea to tax properties in the village if they are not developed? These are private homes that have been in the family for three generations now."

"The council was conned into accepting this in the name of sustainability," responded Clive.

"Only the group that pushed for this doesn't really care about the environment. They only want to control where people live."

A compact SUV cruised by the yard. Hutch waved but drew no response.

"I can't believe that nobody is paying attention to this," exclaimed Hutch.

"Well," replied Clive. "I did talk to Don Lamplighter earlier tonight. He promised me a story. We can at least count on that."

"I doubt that will be enough," added Donaldson while shrugging his shoulders.

Main Street on Victor is also known at Highway 96 and it is a busy thoroughfare containing always-open restaurants and grocery stores. It remained a well- traveled road even for this late at night in this cold.

Clive and his group waved at every vehicle that passed the yard. Any pedestrians that braved the cold were offered a brochure and a cup of hot chocolate.

The gathering had a second purpose of keeping watch to prevent a repeat of Tuesday's night violence, when several downtown businesses had rocks thrown through their windows. Some media outlets interviewed experts that hinted that his group was to blame.

Just after midnight a group of six people; three men and three women walked up to the residence.

The six, who all appeared to be in their early 30s, shook hands with both Donaldson and Hutch.

The pedestrians talked about their trip to the grocery store before Hutch explained the tax and gleefully offered the pamphlets and warm beverages.

The six stayed for about 10 minutes before leaving. Donald was cheerful that they possibly added more members for their cause. That suddenly changed to fear when an explosion rocked the downtown.

Clive bolted out of the residence and instantly recognized the town's favorite establishment,

Downtown Burgers, was ablaze. As a member of the village's volunteer fire department, he raced to the scene.

Along the way he made contact with a state trooper who was already at the fire.

"Somehow I don't think this is going to be good for us," he thought.

Chapter 22

"First, I would like to apologize for how I acted Tuesday night," said Dr. Randall Meyer from his home office Thursday morning. "I acted unprofessionally."

On the other end of the line was Don Lamplighter from his home office.

"Apology accepted," replied Lamplighter. "I look forward to learning more about GEI."

Lamplighter's office was in reality a spare room in the upstairs of his townhouse. It serves four roles - the home of the computer he uses for freelance writing, his workout center, location of Gloria's dresser, and storage area for everything that doesn't fit anywhere else in the 750 square foot residence.

"The environment is an important issue to not only me, but to the entire world," noted Meyer.

"GEI is there to promote the issue."

Meyer's office was the polar opposite of Lamplighter's. The room itself was nearly 300 square feet, nearly one-half of Lamplighter's entire house. Meyer built his office on the first floor of his four-bedroom, three-bath mansion in the wealthy northwest section of Victor.

The room serves only as Meyer's home office.

Lamplighter opened the interview with the question "How did you get involved?"

Lamplighter was conducting the interview in his typical position for every one of his phone stories. He long ago decided that the way for him to get the most accurate quotes was to type along with his subject instead of trying to read his own handwriting. As a result, he conducted this type of interview by crooking his neck to the left for the purpose of holding the phone to his ear. It was most uncomfortable for him, but like anything else that he has been doing for the last couple of years, he needed the money.

"I actually got into it recently compared to everything else I have done regarding the environment," explained Meyer, who spent the next five minutes explaining his history with the movement. "All of this is available on my website at GRIT."

Lamplighter made a note to print out the RIT pages with Meyer's history as Meyer took a relaxed pose - leaning back in his chair with his feet on his desk.

"Anyway," continued Meyer. "As I said, I moved to Victor in order to raise my children in an area that was more environmentally healthy."

Just then one of his grandchildren - a three-year-old boy who was visiting for Christmas, climbed onto his lap.

"To do my part I joined the Victor Green Team," he continued. "They picked me as their leader.

Because of my research and found GEI which coincidently is currently headed by Charles Isadore, a good friend of mine from college."

Lamplighter asked for a spelling of that name for further research.

"Please explain to the readers of the Victor News why you think that GEI is a good investment for the village," asked Lamplighter.

Meyer shooed the child off of his lap before grabbing a pen from his desk and resuming his relaxed position. This time he was taping his pen on the armrest of his chair.

"I looked at the GEI mission and it seemed to be in line with what the Green Team is trying to accomplish," replied Meyer. "Then, once I found out about Isadore's involvement I dug deeper on some of its history and programs."

Meyer spent another seven minutes explaining the history of GEI. Lamplighter had already printed this information from the internet, but he needed a rest for his neck so he let Meyer talk while he stopped typing and took a drink of water.

"I really don't see how anyone could be against this organization unless they didn't care about the environment," he added.

Lamplighter assumed his normal telephone interview position.

"Was there any discussion among the Green Team about the details of the group?" asked

Lamplighter

"There was one question about the $600 monthly fee," noted Meyer. "But no, GEI gives a good overview of the organization. I gave out some promotional brochures and showed a DVD of Isadore talking about its history, goals and future plans. It was a unanimous vote."

Lamplighter had prepared a list of questions. He made a mark on the committee and moved onto the next issue.

"Could you please tell me who the town council had as a liaison at that time?" he questioned.

"It was McDermott," answered Meyer. "But I should say that Reid is an environmentalist and is pushing to take over the spot."

"Have you talked to either of them?" said Lamplighter to continue this line of questions.

"McDermott was at the meeting," replied Meyer. "As you know, he can't vote, but he did voice his approval. I know your next question ... and I have given Reid the brochure and DVD, but he has yet to respond."

'That actually was my next question," noted Lamplighter as he crossed off yet another topic from his list.

"Have you had a chance to review some of the concerns of those protesting GEI in other cities?" inquired Lamplighter.

This question brought Meyer out of his relaxed position into one of a more serious nature. He sat up and pointed at nobody in particular.

"Look I've said this to you on Tuesday in Farmington," he said with a slight hint of annoyance in his voice. "I think that all of these protests are done by a bunch of right-wing nut jobs who are automatically against anything that they think will help the environment."

Meyer stood up and started pacing around the room without interrupting his rant.

"That being said, I've both heard and read that you are a fair reporter that says both sides of an issue that will print my side," he said while walking brisk laps around his desk. "So I'm curious as to what you are going to detail from the other side."

Lamplighter went into detail about the cities and the reason that each group was protesting. The topics ranged from increased taxes and water and electricity rates, to a loss of jobs when a power plant was shut down to the constitutionality of a local government entity entering a deal with a foreign organization.

He could hear the arrogant sighs coming from the other end of the phone connection.

143

"Look, I appreciate you doing your due diligence as a reporter, but those protests are exactly what I thought - right-wing nut jobs," said Meyer, who stopped his pacing. "Ask the readers of the Victor News this ... What is more important to them - Having a clean earth for their children and grandchildren or giving in to a right-wing agenda?"

Meyer then sat back down in his chair and starting taping his pen on his desk.

Lamplighter was not fazed by his response, instead he calmly checked another topic off of his list and referred to his copy of the GEI rules for his last questions.

"Have you read the bylaw that said that GEI wants to control human consumption, production and reproduction in the name of the environment?" he asked.

Meyer laughed. "Now you sound like one of those conspiracy idiots."

Lamplighter read the section, number and letter directly from his printout for Meyer.

"No way, it really says that?" asked Meyer, who took a pause to call up the rules on his computer.

There was a one minute silence when neither Lamplighter nor Meyer spoke.

"I'll have to get back to you on that," said Meyer, who then hung up.

Chapter 23

"I call this a double win for us," said a groggy Charles Isadore.

As he powered up his computer, he eagerly awaited an update on the events in Victor while talking on the telephone with his contact in the areas.

"If it went as well as you said ....," Isadore continued with a yawn, "We should be ready in no time."

"Well click on the link in the email and find out," replied an eager Absalom while watching TV in resort hotel room.

Isadore rubbed the sleep from his eyes.

"How can you sound so good after your party last night?" asked Isadore as he took a sip of a liquid antacid. "Man, I got so wasted, it was great."

"I never even touch alcohol or drugs," responded Absalom as he was reading the crawl under the 24-hour news channel. "I like to keep my mind clear. There is always money to funnel somewhere."

Isadore had hosted his yule holiday event in his house. He stumbled down to his office when

Absalom called.

"That is why you are so popular," added Isadore as he opened the email from his Satan-worshiping friend across Lake Ontario.

Isadore shook his head.

"What do you mean you don't do that stuff?" he yelled. "I was at your Summer Solstice party in

June. It was the best one we've ever had."

"I thank you for that compliment," replied Absalom.

"So what do you mean you don't have fun?" asked Isadore.

Absalom rubbed his escort's back.

"Oh, I didn't say I don't have fun. I had fun all right," he said.

The link led Isadore to a website with two videos.

The first video started playing. It showed a picture of Roger Shawn. The newscaster described him as a member of Citizens Against The Tax. It also noted he was a frequent visitor to the chat rooms of both Dr. Joe Hammill and Gregg Matzek. The video included showed a screen shot of Clive holding a gun.

It cut to a clip from the newly elected mayor of Victor.

"These Citizens Against The Tax must be stopped," she said. "They claim to be saving our village - they are doing nothing but wrecking it."

Isadore paused the video. He stretched and looked around his room as he noticed people from his party stirring. He counted seven people that were so inebriated from Wednesday night's bash that they just crashed on the floor in his office.

"Your bodyguard shot Shawn, making you a hero too," continued Isadore.

Absalom grinned.

"That's why I call that a double win," said Isadore before he played the second half of the video.

It showed the newscaster describing the fire in Victor the previous night and explained that suspects were caught on video and later seen shaking hands with Steve Clive and three other members of Citizens Against The Tax. The talking head added that the group was also suspected in the rock-throwing incident on Tuesday night. It noted that protests are getting increasingly violent in other communities.

The video cut to an interview with Sheriff Cornell.

"If they are around the country, it is a win for you too," Absalom added.

"I call for everyone involved to end the violence and settle this peacefully," said the Sheriff. "Both my department and the state police will add extra patrols in Victor tonight."

Isadore stopped to collect a thought.

"What about Don Lamplighter?" he asked.

"He only works for a weekly so none of his articles have been published," Absalom replied.

"Still, I should find out what he knows."

Absalom's escort rolled over and looked at him with a smile.

"Well, I have some more fun ahead of me," he said and hung up.

Isadore stretched and grinned at the same time.

"I think we have discredited them enough," he said as he closed his laptop.

He sat at his desk drumming his fingers on the armrest of his chair.

"This is working out perfectly," he thought. "We snuck that tax in there as we did in every city that became a member with us."

He looked over at the yule log, which was still burning in his office fireplace.

"We are nothing but a bunch of Satan-worshiping control freaks, but since we say it is in the name of the environment, people buy it," he grinned and stretched again. "Some studies even show that global warming stopped in 1997."

Isadore turned and looked out the window to a snowstorm and laughed.

Chapter 24

Lamplighter continued his busy morning. Thursday, December 22 was a bus-to-work- day which put his morning routine into rush mode.

He finished his interview with Meyer at 11:30 a.m. He followed that by another failed attempt to call his father. The calls left just 45 minutes to shower, have breakfast and get dressed for his shift at Wal-Mart. He did a morning devotional and walked to the bus stop. The bus he took was scheduled to arrive at 12:15 p.m. That line took him to the main terminal area in downtown Canandaigua. The bus that takes him to Wal-Mart arrives at the store at 1:15 p.m. It is 45 minutes earlier than when his shift starts, but it is better than the next option, arriving late. Lamplighter went up to his bedroom. The window from that room offered the best view of the parking lot of his townhouse complex. He did this every morning during the colder times in the central New York community.

"Whew," he sighed. "At least I don't have to shovel snow too."

His devotional was Psalm 72, which told of Christ receiving gifts, a prophecy that was fulfilled in the New Testament accounts.

Lamplighter showered. He took the opportunity to practice singing the song that the town's combined choir was going to sing at the concert Saturday. It was a medley and he only got two looks at it from Sunday morning practices.

He efficiently used his dry-off time to check his email. Lamplighter first looked at his personal account. It had 10 entries in his inbox - five were spam trying to either sell him products or try to trick him into giving his savings to some guy in Nigeria. The other five were e-cards offering Christmas greetings.

Lamplighter then checked his work account. There were three messages.

The first was from the editor of the Victor News.

"How many stories are you planning on doing?" he asked.

"Count on three," replied Lamplighter. "One with a follow up on the town council and what is going to happen next, one a basic overview of the Farmington Town Council and one on the violence and Citizens Against The Tax. They claim they are not involved."

The next he checked was from Steve Clive.

"Sorry If I'm bugging you too much, but it wasn't us," he said again.

Lamplighter replied. "Not a problem. I appreciate you keeping me informed, but I actually have to get to my other job. Talk to you later."

Could you please relay this to the Sheriff's Department with your explanation of events?"

The third was from the editor of Maranatha Monthly offering a couple of assignments for January.

"Of course, I look forward to them, God bless you," responded Lamplighter.

Lamplighter then sent off one email each to attorney Connors and Councilman Cooper to find out what the town council is going to do next as four of its five voting members were killed Monday.

He shut down his computer and dragged himself down the stairs for breakfast. Lamplighter made sure not to step on his meowing cat as he got into the kitchen. He made himself a bowl of cereal by combining one half generic raisin bran and one half some generic sugar-coated flakes.

Lamplighter grabbed a banana, then went into the living room and turned on the TV as he started to eat. He switched the channel to the 24-hour news. It was on the middle segments, which talked about sports, weather and features. He chowed down as fast as he could while the cat was studying him closely, eagerly awaiting some scraps, which he never gave.

Given the time crunch, he got dressed, leaving the news on so he could watch the main stories at noon. Lamplighter raced upstairs, put on his uniform and quickly got back into the living room.

He collected his knife and work earpiece as he watched.

The first segment offered exactly the same information as the clip that Absalom sent to Isadore.

"Yeah, that was predictable." Lamplighter made a mental note to look at the chat areas on both Matzek's and Dr. Hammill's websites just to confirm that Shawn was participating in those.

Next was the report on the fire last night. Lamplighter paid close attention since he hadn't heard about this before. The report included the same quotes from the Victor mayor and Steve Clive.

"OK this story just got a lot longer," he thought has he put on his winter boots.

Next on was the world news, which included more reports of natural disasters and national reports with notes on where the presidential election candidates were campaigning. Lamplighter listened as he put on his jacket, checked his pockets to make sure he had everything he needed for his shift at Wal- Mart, pet the cat, and walked out the door to his bus stop.

Chapter 25

The TV news was also on at Bob's sub shop.

"Wow," thought Glass. "They didn't even talk about me."

After the rough night, Steve Clive set his alarm for noon just so he could watch the news. The hope was that he could find out what was being said about his group and plan his next move.

"Oh no," Clive said. "I think we have just been set up."

He recorded the segment of himself shaking hands with the people who were caught on video setting fire to the hot dog stand. Clive stopped it frame by frame.

"Just as I thought," he said, " I don't know those people at all."

The station stopped the video at one frame and witnessed the group taking brochures from him.

"Great ... that is the last thing we need," he thought as he rubbed his chin in disgust. "I can see how this is going already. Just like with the shooter, they will find an apartment, claim things they find there were used in the hot dog stand fire and tell everyone that they found brochures from us."

Clive sat forward in his chair with his head on his hands.

"How are you doing Honey?" the voice of his wife Edith came from the kitchen. "How about some soup and sandwiches?".

"Sound great," he replied, then put his head back in his hands.

The tax was an important fight for him. Clive had spent his life building a construction business.

He garnered an excellent reputation for honesty and hard work. Clive and his wife also spent time volunteering in Victor. They were active members of the local Baptist church and worked together to form a community garden club.

The Clives saved their money wisely, earning enough to purchase a 1.5 acre property within the village limits. The goal was to keep the estate up so their four children would have a nest egg.

Part of the planning included setting aside some money to afford the taxes on the property. The sustainability tax would change all of that. The village and school taxes would stay the same, but the extra town clause that started on January 1 was set to punish the landowners in the village.

The law levied an extra tax on any land that was more than one-half acre, but that would be waived if the property was developed. Since the Clives' land was more than an acre, that fine doubled.

The net effect is that the Clives would have to give up the estate that they felt they earned.

Steve and Edith got together with other landowners in the city in an effort to stop the tax.

The stated goal of those who promoted the tax was to centralize the population by increasing number of people in the village and leave more undeveloped land in other areas of the town.

"I don't understand why they would do this," he mumbled.

The couple took a break from the fight to enjoy their lunch.

"It's lucky for us that the media has not arrived on our property yet," said Edith.

"I agree," replied Steve. "We might not be able to keep this land for long, but for now it serves as a great respite for us."

A phone call broke that rest. The caller ID noted that it was from George Donaldson.

"Steve you two better get down to my house," he said. "There are some people that want to meet you."

Steve and Edith arrived at the Donaldson's Main Street home. The group had decided to keep the vigil going there. This shift was manned by housewife Mary Black, her teenage daughter Alicia, Tom Stark, a 50-year-old realtor and Ed Overton, a 20-something barista who had the day off from the downtown coffee shop.

As the group was talking inside, the four-person crew was growing. Another family of four - a father, mother and two children - arrived to help.

"Word is getting out," said the father. "We live in Rochester and learned that we are part of GEI as well. I decided to take time out from running my restaurant to come here and help."

Chapter 26

Once again Don Lamplighter found himself purposely standing outside in sub-zero temperatures.

The goal this time was to catch his bus.

"Man, I love this," he said to the older lady who had just arrived at the bus stop.

She looked at him like he was crazy. Given his abnormal affinity for cold temperatures, she had a point.

The bus arrived on time.

"Cold enough for you?" the driver joked as she opened the door.

Lamplighter let the woman on first. He got on next giving the bus driver his $1 fare.

"Let me guess," said the driver upon recognizing Lamplighter. "It's not cold enough for you."

Lamplighter chuckled as the door was shut and the driver set off on the seven-block trip to the downtown station. Once there, Lamplighter made small talk for five minutes until it was time to board his bus to Wal-Mart. The station was busy as four bus lines were scheduled to depart at 12:30 p.m.

Lamplighter typically waits for the rest of the passengers to board before he gets on. He takes whatever seat is available.

Today's driver is Mitch, a former Wal-Mart employee that left to take the bus driver job.

Lamplighter ends up on his route about twice a week.

"This bus goes to Victor," Mitch jested.

Lamplighter just looked down and shook his head.

"Merry Christmas!" Lamplighter responded as he took a seat right behind the driver.

"With all that is happening there I don't think you want to go there anyway," added Mitch as he pulled away from the station.

"I might have to go there anyway" said Lamplighter. "I have two stories to write and I have to find out what is going on."

'That's right you work up there," replied Mitch when they got to the next stop. "But why is it two stories?"

"Good question," Lamplighter said. "I have one about the shooting from Monday to find out what happens next with the council and one on the tax itself."

'Tax?" questioned Mitch.

He explained the situation to Mitch as the route took him past the hospital on the way to the highway that frontages Wal-Mart.

"So it's kind of like a 1776 thing?" said Mitch.

"You know I never thought of it that way," added Lamplighter.

He sat back in his seat and pondered what his friend had said.

The two exchanged Christmas greetings when Lamplighter left the bus for work.

Lamplighter was undisturbed all the way into the break room. He immediately found a spot next to a stack of daily papers. He read four articles, but found nothing new other than an extended interview with the Victor mayor. Lamplighter tried to call her, left a message asking for an interview of his own on Friday. He took note that the protests in other cities were getting as violent and that some city leaders were calling for martial law.

"If Clive is right, it's a huge set up," he thought.

He couldn't help but notice that the events in Victor were the topic of discussion at two of the room's eight tables. Lamplighter had an idea. He would keep track of the conversations just to see what side everybody is taking. Just before he left the room, Lamplighter tallied eight speakers, all of whom were against the Citizens Against The Tax.

Lamplighter met department manager Regis as he walked to the garden center, or seasonal as it is known for the holidays, where he worked. The area had been decorated for Christmas since October. Lamplighter's job was to condense the area down to get ready for the post-Christmas rush and the spring season.

He continued his experiment with the customers as he performed his assigned tasks. Lamplighter's running total was 16 people talking about the Victor events with 14 against the protesters and two expressing understanding for the group but disagreeing with the tactics.

He grabbed a cup of coffee during his break and sat on the sidelines in the break room. Lamplighter heard two more of his coworkers hurling insults regarding the protesters. They both agreed with using martial against them and taking their guns away.

Lamplighter operated the register for 17 customers between his afternoon break and lunch break.

"You are Don Lamplighter right?" asked one customer at around 5 p.m. "What do you think of what is going on in Victor?"

It was the first person that asked him directly about the situation since he left the bus.

"I don't know yet," he replied.

"Well aren't you writing stories about it?" continued the insistent customer.

"I will, but I have to check things out first," he replied. "I have some interviews slated for tomorrow. I will know then."

The customer got into his car and immediately made a phone call.

"He claims not to know anything," said Julius.

"Of course he does," replied Absalom from his office. "Did he talk about Victor at all?"

"He said that he has some interviews tomorrow," replied Julius. "Then he claimed he will have more information."

"OK," said a happy Absalom. "Keep your eye on him."

Lamplighter headed to the break room for lunch. His running total was 20 people against the protesters, the same two questioning the tactics and just two supporters.

He sat for his lunch and coffee and pondered the reasons why as he waited for the 6:30 p.m. news broadcast.

Chapter 27

Jacob Glass faced a dilemma.

Glass spent last night sound asleep before being rudely awakened by his alarm clock. He went to work, spending nearly all of his time keeping the busy restaurant clean.

"OK, now what do I do?" he asked as he returned to his apartment and sat on his couch.

He stared into space looking at the clock. It was only 5:15. Glass got up and started stomping around his apartment.

"What do I do? What do I do?" he muttered.

The busy work schedule gave him a good workout. This had the effect of clearing his mind out somewhat. He started thinking more clearly than usual.

Glass stopped to stare out the window at his black Neon.

"OK let's review," he thought as he started more laps around his couch.

His first thoughts were a play-by-play of the fight with Lamplighter.

"Man I hate Lamplighter," he growled.

Glass finished that thought just as he ended up looking at his car.

"I took that to Victor Monday night," he smiled, "but according to the news, the place is filled with cops now. That won't work again."

He started stomping around the room again. This time he thought about Tuesday night and his successful theft of the kettle at the downtown drug. Glass got to his window and started another staring contest with an inanimate object. He shook his head.

"Probably shouldn't push it for a third time," he thought and started walking around his couch, this time in the opposite direction.

He paused to look at his clock. It was now 5:25. Glass shook his head again as he recalled the events from Wednesday night.

"An old man at a strip mall where nobody goes, that was easy," he thought. "I should risk that as tonight's target."

He looked out the window.

"Looks like I'm going to need you again," he said to his car and headed out on his mission.

On a whim Glass decided to scout a drug store that was on a frontage road. It was located halfway between his place and the strip mall.

"Curious," he thought.

What Glass noticed was that the store had an unusual entrance and therefore a potential easy target.

"That lady is standing in front of her kettle," he observed. "If I play this right ..."

Glass quickly formulated his plan and then executed it flawlessly.

He backed up into the spot right next to the bell ringer.

"How lucky can I be?" he wondered.

The next step was to open the car door. Glass unbuckled his seatbelt and pretended to look for something in his car as he watched the ringer.

That is when he heard a loud crash coming from the other side of the parking lot. He didn't care what it was, but it did draw the attention of everyone and left the red kettle unguarded.

Glass leaped out of his car, grabbed the pot, threw it into the passenger seat and dove into his driver's spot. He was gone before anyone noticed the money was missing.

"Wow, not even Lamplighter could have kept me from this one," he thought as he got to the stop sign.

Glass then burst out in laughter as he looked into his rearview mirror. Facing the store was an expensive sports car covered with a huge pile of snow and an empty spot on the roof right above it.

He continued to his favorite hidden alley in the abandoned industrial area and took his bolt cutters to the pot. He kissed the glob of dollars that he grabbed out of the pot. The grand total of his haul was $215.85.

Glass gave the money another kiss as he set forth to his favorite park for his favorite dealer and another hit of meth. He stopped at the deli for dinner before going home for his fix.

Chapter 28

The 6:30 p.m. TV news report was just what Lamplighter feared. The situation in Victor was getting worse.

Lamplighter expected to see a summation of the events from last night combined with background information on the rock throwing from Tuesday. What he watched was a live report on the events with even more people rushed into the area.

"Victor is shaping up for a violent night again as the number of protesters in the downtown area of the village keeps growing," said the newscaster while standing in front of town hall. "From just my vantage point alone, I can count about 100 people lining Main Street from here to Dunkin Donuts restaurant on the other end of the downtown area."

The video then showed a scan of the road to show the mass that gathered on the sidewalks of the entire one-mile stretch of the busy state highway.

"According to the Victor mayor, the crowd started gathering at dusk and has been growing ever since," said the bundled-up man holding the microphone. "There have been some reports of small fires and some eggs being thrown at luxury cars and village owned vehicles, but that has yet to be confirmed."

One of Lamplighter's co-workers scoffed.

"Typical conservatives," she said before continuing a conversation at a table with three other friends.

Lamplighter said nothing, instead trying to concentrate on the news, which had been showing still shots of the buildings that were boarded up after Tuesday's violence. The next cut was to the restaurant that burned down the night before.

Next up was a pan of the inside of the atrium of one of the downtown buildings.

"This area was supposed to be filled tonight for the village's annual sing along, but the mayor has decided to cancel the event because of the violence," said the voiceover.

The news then showed an empty chair set up in the center of the atrium.

"There is no word on whether Santa Claus is going to show up here tomorrow night as promised," he added.

"Perfect," said Isadore as he leaned back in his GEI office while watching the news over the internet.

Another shot of the downtown area focused on a county sheriff patrol car taking a slow drive past a house.

"This started when a group known as Citizens Against The Tax started a 24-hour vigil in front of this house," noted the anchor man. "It is the Main

169

Street home and real estate business group member George Donaldson. No members of the group agreed to be on camera for this report."

The next interview was that of Victor's Mayor Jill Watson. She was standing with Cooper in front of the village hall, which is across from town hall.

"I can assure you that both the Sheriff's Department and state police have assured me that they will increase patrols to protect the citizens of Victor," said the mayor. "I have also called the Governor in advance to notify him I might ask him to activate the National Guard if this gets out of hand."

The coworker scoffed again.

"Good we need to arrest all of these idiots," she said as the rest of table laughed. "They are filled with so much hate."

Lamplighter was distracted by Mike, a greeter and frequent tablemate, who sat next to him.

"What do you think of all of this?" asked Mike.

"I'm going to find out," said Lamplighter as he took out his cell phone.

His first call was to Salvation Army Captain Irving to arrange a plan to ring bells Friday morning.

"You know the news was just talking about that guy who robs bell ringers?" inquired Mike. 'Police still can't figure this out."

"Shoot, I missed that," responded Lamplighter.

His next call was to Professor Meyer. He left a message to see if he had found out anything else about GEI. Lamplighter then left a text for Gloria noting that he was going to Victor tonight. He looked up and made a mental note that other cites that had protest movements against GEI were experienced similar types of violence. Finally he sent a text to the Victor News editor to tell him of his plans.

Lamplighter finished the rest of his shift. He found it depressing with Christmas just three nights away, the decorations that he had fun building, had been taken apart and sold. He spent the next two hours waiting on the bevy of customers that were getting in their last-minute shopping. Any time between checkouts was spent cleaning the area.

He watched the news again during his 9:30 p.m. break. The reporter noted that more people were gathered on the streets, but as yet there wasn't any violence, but that the crowd was getting bigger and louder.

"Well, that's good," Lamplighter thought as he took a sip of coffee – "at least for now."

His cell phone buzzed as Gloria responded to his text.

"I guess we should check it out," she said.

Lamplighter finished his break. He finished his shift with one hour of cleaning, all the while trying to cheer himself up by humming Christmas carols. His phone was buzzing as he slid his card through the reader to end his shift. Gloria was waiting for him at the door.

"Christmas, downtown Victor, our sleep," said Gloria.

"I know," replied Don, "Three things that are being ruined by the riots. I was thinking of giving the same clue."

The couple went home so he could get his camera, recorder and notebook. He also filled a bottle of water for himself and grabbed a soda for Gloria.

"I need to see this for myself," Don said to Gloria as they headed for Victor.

Chapter 29

"Oh no," said Steve Clive as he sat on the steps of the Donaldson's house at 11 p.m. "This is not what I wanted."

No matter where he looked in downtown Victor there was utter chaos.

"Who are these people and what are they doing here?" he asked Donaldson who sat next to him.

"All I wanted to do is save this village," he said while raising his arms in the air in disgust. "Instead it looks like I brought its destruction."

Edith Clive sat on the steps on the other side of Steve.

"You know that you had nothing to do with this," she said, putting her arm around her husband.

"We just had a small group that was protesting a tax that makes no sense. Besides we don't know any of these people."

The Donaldson house sits at the T- intersection of Main Street and Church Street. Across the street to the west is a pizza place that has a parking lot that borders the town hall. A Methodist Church is across the street to the south. From the second story window the Donaldsons can look west and see most of downtown. The intent was to use the view as a place to spot any crimes that may be done in their name.

"Well there's no point in that anymore," said Donaldson's granddaughter Jenny as she came down from her shift at the window. "There are so many things going on that I can't possibly report them all. Plus there are so many cops here that they will probably find it first anyway."

Jenny sat on the porch and pouted.

"The tax seems irrelevant now," said Steve as he rubbed his chin. "This village is being destroyed. I will be dead before the city recovers from this."

An anonymous college-aged looking man approached Steve.

"Steve Clive right?" he asked.

"Yes," replied Steve.

"Woohoo!" yelled the man, who promptly shook Steve's hand, "Woohoo!"

The man then ran away, threw a brick through the window of the pizza place and turned around to point at the group on the porch.

"Woohoo!" he yelled as he ran away back toward the village center.

The Clives and Donaldsons had weapons on them for self-defense but all they did was sit back and watch for fear of further escalating the conflict and having even more blame placed on them.

Following the hooligan led the group's eyes downtown where they saw fires and throngs of people looting the drug store, library and hobby store. A line of police had formed to get ready to move in on the protestors, Edith looked north on Church Street to the residential area of the village.

"At least they haven't been up there yet," she said as Steve put his arm around her.

Lamplighters arrived at 11:45 p.m. and were stuck at a sheriff-manned check point.

"Sorry, nobody but residents allowed past this point," he said, "too dangerous."

"I'm not dangerous," laughed Don. "I'm from the Victor News."

"Dangerous for you, not the village," replied the deputy, one whom Don did not recognize.

Don texted to a speed dial number on his cell phone.

"What if I just park at the small church on top of the hill and walk from there?" asked Don.

"Believe me, you are not the first person to suggest that," replied the deputy as a message for him came over his radio.

The deputy looked at the couple.

"The sheriff said I could let you in," replied the deputy, who talked on his radio again.

"He suggested you go down and park at the Methodist Church on Main Street.

"Thank you," said Gloria as she drove off.

"Wow," exclaimed Don. "Even closer than I expected."

The Lamplighters didn't need to look far to find action. Don interviewed people on the streets.

He recorded conversations with 12 protesters and found it curious that only two were actually from Victor.

Gloria took photos of the holes in the town hall windows and a couch that was thrown on the street and set on fire. She got a group shot of eight people who appeared to be in their mid-20s as they posed for her while wearing Citizens Against The Tax shirts. Gloria turned away when one of them aimed an obscene gesture at her.

"Hey," he said as he charged at her. "I didn't say you were done."

Don stepped in front of his wife. "I said she is done," he replied.

The Clives and one of the deputies approached to intervene. Seeing this, the protestor threw a rock at Don, who swatted it away with his cane.

The incident convinced them that they should leave after only 15 minutes at the scene. They crossed the street to talk with the Donaldson/Clive group. Gloria took a group photo as they talked.

The Lamplighters headed for Canandaigua at 12:15 a.m.

"I can't believe this is going on here," remarked Gloria. "So close to our home."

"That's not all that worries me," sighed Don. "I wonder what is going to happen next. How are politicians going to play this for their gain?"

They were silent for several miles until Gloria drove the Neon onto Highway 332 for the trip back. They both let out a sigh.

"Buffalo, Watertown and Toronto," said Don.

"I can guess this one," replied Gloria, "three cities where the protesters came from."

"Yep," said Don followed by a short pause. "That is why I am worried about what will happen next. If none of the people are from here, it means that they don't really care about Victor. What does that mean for the people that live there?"

The Lamplighters wound down by heating some canned beef stew and watching a Christmas movie disguised as a love story.

Don had Gloria pick out the nightly Bible devotional. Her random selection was Revelation

Chapter 2, both of them noted the positive thought of Verse 23. "And the city had no need of the sun, neither the moon, to shine in it; for the glory of God did lighten it and the lamb is the light there of."

"Well that sounds a lot better than what we saw tonight," Gloria remarked as she climbed into bed. Don went to do download the photos and transcribe the notes from his interviews.

Chapter 30

"Why did you request this location?" asked Captain Irving as he set up a ringing stand in front of the drug store Friday morning in downtown Victor. "After the violence here in Victor, I didn't think anyone would want to ring downtown here."

"Excellent question," replied Lamplighter. "I figure I have some work to do here today anyway. I might as well do it this morning and get all of my interviews in while I am here."

The two discussed the Old Testament verses that the captain had suggested. Lamplighter added that he had started reading the New Testament account of Christ's birth starting with Matthew Chapter 1, Verse 23. "Behold a virgin shall be with child and shall bring forth a son and they shall call his name Emmanuel, which being interpreted is God with us."

Lamplighter then grabbed the bell and looked around at the remains of the fires and vandalism from the last couple nights of what were called protests.

"OK, but as part of the deal the district major wants you out at dark, so 4:30 p.m." reminded

Captain Irving. "I will pick you up."

Captain Irving started toward the church van then turned around.

179

"So what do you think of all of this?" he asked.

"Something isn't right about it," replied Lamplighter. "I have a lot of questions I want answered.

That is why I am here I want to see how this starts."

It was 9:30 a.m. and Lamplighter realized that he had better get going on both reasons that he is here - ring bells and watch for clues to the riots. He had the day off from Wal-Mart and was going to ring bells today anyway, so he signed up for the kettle in downtown Victor. He started with his version of "Let It Snow" followed by "Away In A Manger."

"Thank you for coming here," said the first person to donate, a 30-ish woman with a child in a stroller. "I'm glad that we didn't scare you off."

"Merry Christmas," was Lamplighter's reply.

There were some teenagers leaving the library who stopped by right after her. Each of the three donated a dollar.

"Hi, I'm Don Lamplighter from the Victor news," said Lamplighter, "Could I please take a moment of your time to ask you some questions?"

The three teenagers stopped.

"OK question one," started Lamplighter. "Were any of you at the protest last night?"

The teens shook their heads, confirming that they were not.

"OK," Lamplighter continued even though he didn't quite believe the first answer. "Do you know of anyone who was?"

The teens looked at each other and again shook their heads in the negative.

"Finally," asked Lamplighter. "Were any of you invited?"

One of the teens, a tall young woman wearing a Victor Central School letter jacket, finally spoke.

"We were talking about that last night," she said, noting that school was canceled due to riots.

"We were watching it on TV. We didn't know anything about it until the news." "Thank you for your time," said Lamplighter as the teens walked away.

Lamplighter collected his thoughts as he took a sip of coffee. The area was in the middle of a warming trend with an expected high of 25 degrees. It was cold, but not cold enough to keep people in a northern city off the streets.

That brought Lamplighter to a point.

"Where did everyone go?" he asked himself as he again examined the parking lot. "I recognize some of the people around here, but it is not enough for a protest as big as last night."

Lamplighter put his coffee mug on the ground.

"So if what the teens are saying is true," he thought. "Then people are being brought in here. If that is so, who is bringing them ... and why?"

His phone started vibrating.

"Where do they have you now?" asked Gloria in the text.

"Downtown Victor," he replied. "I just thought of this morning. Sorry for not telling you."

"Why did you go there?" she asked.

"I want to be here if anything starts," he noted, then replied with an immediate text.

"The rules say the captain is going to pick me up at 4:30 p.m."

"Oh good," she replied. "See you tonight."

That reminded Lamplighter to make his phone calls. He first left a message with Professor

Meyer. He set up a 1 p.m. lunch break with Mayor Watson and a 2 p.m. get together with Steve

Clive. Sheriff Cornell noted that he was going to be in Victor at 4 p.m. and they could get together then. Town attorney Connors promised an email with the rules for forming a new town council.

Clive's grand-daughter Jenny stopped by on the way to the drug store. She noted that she was going to stop by later with Donaldson.

Lamplighter did not keep track of people donating to the kettle, but he guessed that it was more than he expected. What he did not see were protesters gathering in the square.

"I wonder what that means?" he asked himself.

Lamplighter enjoyed the next hour and 45 minutes of singing and ringing bells.

"I like the fact that you are a fair reporter," said Watson as she walked up to donate at the kettle.

'Thanks," replied Lamplighter. "I would like to get your side of this."

He hid the kettle behind the pharmacy desk of the drug store and used the restroom before meeting Watson at a small coffee shop across the street from his ringing post.

"So you wanted to know what I think of this," said the mayor as the waiter placed two cups of coffee on the table. "I think it is all the fault of Steve Clive and his citizens group."

Lamplighter already had his recorder on, but took pen and paper notes as well.

"He claims that he didn't want a big protest like this and didn't invite those people here," he noted. He started this," she replied, "Everyone is here because of him.''

Lamplighter's roast beef melt arrived. He took a bite and a sip of coffee before continuing his interview.

"So is the tax real?" he asked.

"Yes," was Mayor Watson's quick reply, "and to follow up on that, I support it 100%. We need to clean up the environment and Victor is going to be an example of that."

She took a sip of her coffee.

"Think globally, act locally," she added.

"Would you really call for the governor to impose martial law?" he asked.

Mayor Watson put down her sandwich.

"You bet I would," she added. "These people are destroying our fantastic village. If the State Police and Sheriff can't stop Clive and his group that is the next step."

Lamplighter noticed that his break was almost over. He thanked Watson for the interview and wrapped the rest of his sandwich to put it in his pocket. He then got the bell and tripod for his afternoon ringing session. Clive, Donaldson and Jenny were waiting for him.

Clive and Donaldson took turns denying starting the riots as Lamplighter finished his sandwich since it was still warm. He got their rants on tape and looked forward to listening to them later.

"I got something to show you," said Jenny as soon as the group founders finished. "I recognize one of the protesters."

She noted that she is a sophomore at St. Lawrence University in Canton, New York and brought out a yearbook. Jenny pointed to a photo of a student, A.J. Fephi, who was with her in the international relations club.

"This guy came up to us, shook Steve's hand and threw a rock at the pizza place across the street," she said. "He got kicked out of college, but before that, he told me at one of our college group meetings that he is the Mayor's nephew. He is not even from Victor, he is from someplace in New York City."

"Interesting," replied Don, who took out his camera and took a picture of the page. "Let's show this to Sheriff Cornell. He is going to be here to talk to me at 4 p.m."

Lamplighter rang bells for another hour with nothing out of the ordinary happening. He took a restroom break at 2:30 p.m. and came back to find eight young people lining Main Street.

He was curious as to how they got there. His question was soon satisfactorily answered as a van pulled up, eight more people got out and the van immediately took off. Lamplighter wrote down the license plate and noted that the van had a St. Lawrence University student parking sticker and an ad from a car dealer in Brooklyn.

On the third stop, eight more people got out. Lamplighter also identified the driver as the student from the yearbook.

The drop-off system continued until Lamplighter counted a good 80 people on the sidewalk.

Another van showed up to help. He wrote down that license plate also. Lamplighter then noted that the second van's dealer ad was from Canandaigua.

"OK, that mystery is solved," he said to himself as Sheriff Cornell approached.

"This is going to be a rough night again," said Cornell as he put a few coins in the pot.

"Maybe not," replied Lamplighter as he explained how he saw the crowd grow.

Clive, Donaldson and Jenny approached and explained their story to Cornell.

"I'm going to have to investigate this," said Cornell as he looked at Lamplighter. "I'm sure you are going to as well."

Captain Irving showed up on time to take Lamplighter home. Irving and Lamplighter were talking about Saturday's concert as Jenny was pointing to the student. Lamplighter took off his apron as he observed the sheriff and another deputy put the student under arrest. He managed to get a quick photo and jotted down some information before heading off for band and choir practice. In the background the National Guard was starting to assemble and the people that called themselves protestors trying to scatter away.

"Whew," thought Lamplighter. "That could have been a disaster."

Chapter 31

"You lied to me," said Professor Meyer.

He was sitting in his office looking at a stack of papers he accumulated in his research of GEI.

"Don Lamplighter was right," he said.

Charles Isadore was on the other end of the phone. He was sitting in his office answering emails from GEI members from around the world.

"How can I help you my friend?" replied Isadore, trying to remain calm.

"I am definitely not your friend," retorted the angry Meyer. "You guys are a bunch of Satan-worshipping liars."

Isadore leaned forward in his chair to rest his elbows on his desk.

"We want to make sure that we fix the world's environmental problems," said Isadore, who sounded like he was regurgitating rehearsed lines.

"Cut that crap," replied Meyer as he started stomping around him office, making him look like Jacob Glass. "I read your bylaws."

Isadore drummed his fingers on his desk.

"Yes there are many important steps to take in order to save our Earth," said Isadore, whose voice finally displayed a hint of frustration. "I have brought the evidence and reason against you and you do nothing but emotional blackmail and insults. I fell for that once, and I am embarrassed that I actually tried to trick people the same way."

Meyer sat to watch the TV. It was the 24-hour news channel's coverage of the incident in Victor.

"Isn't it important to save the environment?" asked Isadore, now with beads of sweat developing on his forehead. "You are an important part of that fight."

Meyer shook the phone for a while before answering.

"Now that I know the truth, it is so frustrating to talk to you" he said after calming down.

Isadore looked out the window at the snow.

"I find it frustrating that the people don't care about the environment," he replied.

"See there you go again," shouted Meyer. "Lamplighter, those protesters at all of those cities and all of those websites are correct. You are just a bunch of Satan worshipers who have added your takeover agenda to the environmental movement."

"Those people just don't care about the environment," said Isadore with his fingers crossed.

"Yeah, yeah, blah, blah, blah", sighed Meyer. "Your bylaws give you away ... population location control, reproductive control, it's all here."

Isadore was silent as he looked at the caller ID and did a quick web search for information on what his friend Meyer was doing lately.

"There are a lot of crazy conspiracy theorists out there who will say anything," said Isadore, who now grabbed a pencil and started tapping it on the desk. "You can't believe everything you hear.

Remember there were people who believed that the Earth was flat and believed that cigarettes don't cause cancer ... don't get me going about those idiotic climate change deniers. You are smarter than them."

Mayer became irate and grabbed his television remote control with the intent of throwing it, instead he turned on the TV. He grabbed a bit of smile when the national news told stories of other cities where there are protests, then stopped when it was mentioned that they have turned violent and some governors had called out the National Guard to take control.

"More rhetorical exercise," replied Meyer. "I am going to expose this fraud in the name of real environmentalists."

"The people of the world need to know how important the Earth is," remarked Isadore, "for the sake of your children, GEI is here to get that message to them."

Meyer looked at the TV again. The newscast featured a picture of Steve Clive.

"For the sake of my children I am going to help Don Lamplighter expose GEI," said a stern

Meyer. "And I know just how I'm going to do it."

He slammed the receiver the receiver down.

Isadore called up his computer's rolodex and dialed the phone.

"How are you doing my friend in Rochester" he asked as Absalom answered. "I was hoping you can help me out with a couple of problems."

Chapter 32

Jacob Glass didn't have time to go back to his apartment.

He came to a dark realization. Today was Friday the 23rd. According to the bell ringers that he had spoken with, it was the last day that the Salvation Army was collecting with kettles which left him with only one option.

"I will have to get two kettles today," he thought as he was cleaning up a table after a young professional couple left the restaurant.

He thought about the consequences all day long. His previous thefts had given him some cash leftover for him which he can use to get drugs for probably another two weeks.

"What am I going to do after that?" he thought during his break. "No more kettles to take, no more free cash for my stash."

Glass swept the seating area after the lunch crowd left the sandwich shop. The news was on in the background, but it was mostly talking about the events in Victor, the weather and sports.

"No sign of me is a good thing," he thought while taking out a bag full of garbage.

Glass went back to clean every table. It was now 3 p.m. and he had two hours to plan how he was going to accomplish getting two kettles on the same day.

He reviewed the locations he scouted, the methods he used to get each one and how he could get away.

The first conclusion Glass reached is that he would have to go after a place where he had already stolen some money. "They would not expect me there," he thought.

His second was that he needed to find a place on a main road. "For a quick getaway," he said quietly while out on his last smoke break.

He got into his car and headed to Highways 5 & 20, which by his count held four bell ringers.

Glass again surmised that he would not get away with taking either of the two kettles from Wal-Mart due to the amount of people that were there. That left the drug store, where he lucked out in a theft of an unguarded kettle on Thursday and the strip mall, where he gotten away Wednesday thanks to his mace.

"The best part of that," he thought as he took left from Main Street onto the highway, is that I can take the back road out and end up by the factories for the opening."

Glass decided that he was going to get some beer for the night. He went to the drug store in yet a third strip mall on the highway and found a big surprise - a bell ringer alone in front of a nearby liquor store.

"Wow," said Glass as he sized up the petite woman.

Glass pulled his black Neon across the road from the ringer and jumped out of the door with the engine running. He took off at a brisk walk across the roadway to the ringer, donned his weaponized glove, punched the woman in the face and took the kettle. Glass sprinted back to his car and drove off to the strip mall.

"I'm lucky again," he thought as he steered the car toward his next target.

Glass listened to Christmas music as he took a left into the strip mall parking lot and found a smallish, older-looking standing by the kettle. "Same as before," he thought as he pulled up.

He used a similar series of steps to steal this one - leave the car running, dash out of the Neon, hit the ringer with his homemade glove weapon, run back to the car and take off.

Glass got away by driving behind the mall and outlying grocery store to Highway 10. He took another left, then another left at the next intersection. A quick right from there and he was on his way to the abandoned industrial park.

"Whew," he sighed as he opened both kettles. His total was $346. 58.

"This should do for a while," he said as he spread the bills against the steering wheel and gave them a kiss.

He drove into the parking lot of Baker Park, only to find a black limo waiting for him.

Chapter 33

"You mean to say that both of your targets are in the same restaurant?" said Vic from Absalom's mansion in Rochester. "Well, just watch them for now while I decide what to do."

Vic's goons were staking out Professor Meyer as he was having a cup of coffee at the Village Restaurant in downtown Canandaigua. They contacted Vic as soon as Don Lamplighter limped into the scene.

Meyer had final returned Lamplighter's calls.. Both agreed that they should meet in public. He had never been there before, but it was within walking distance. Since Gloria had the family's one working car at her work, Lamplighter picked this place to get together. Meyer and the van full of goons that was following him arrived first. Lamplighter, who had yet to be found by Vic's team, got to the restaurant three minutes after that.

Much to the delight of Lamplighter, he ran into his discus coach Daniel who was coming out of the restroom. After exchanging Christmas greetings, Lamplighter searched the place for

Professor Meyer. Before finding him, he spotted the family of high school football coach Mike Wheeler as well as two fellow Wal-Mart employees.

Lamplighter finally found Meyer and sat across from him.

"So what do you have to tell me?" he asked while pulling out his recorder.

Lamplighter recorded Meyer's nearly five-minute rant before getting a question in edgewise.

The conversation was broken up as the waitress asked for an order. Lamplighter got a coffee and a patty melt. Meyer went with a more elaborate meal of a turkey dinner and water.

"So what is your next step?" asked Lamplighter, again turning on the recorder.

"I haven't thought of that," replied Meyer. "But I am changing the 'Green Team' for sure."

"Well, that is worth a story right there," Lamplighter added.

"I am definitely joining the fight against GEI," noted Meyer. "The story on this is the first step to

That end. Next I'm going to Victor to help Steve Clive."

Lamplighter took a sip of coffee to wash down a bite of his sandwich.

"What do you think of all that?" Lamplighter asked. "I find it strange."

A hungry Meyer took several bites of his mashed potatoes before answering.

"You know what," he answered. "Clive and his group were called every name you can think of, but in the end they proved to be right about the tax."

Lamplighter took a sip of water this time. It gave him time to see that Mitch the bus driver had entered the place also.

"I'm kind of embarrassed that I missed that," said Lamplighter. "All of this happened before I started working there."

The two finished their meals. They each paid their own bill and walked out the door. The next thing Lamplighter knew there was a black bag being placed over his head.

"You are finally going to get shut up," said one of the goons.

Lamplighter felt punches hit both sides of his face and arms. He guessed that he had two attackers. Normally he would be able to put up a decent defense, but with his eyes covered there was nothing he could do but wait for an opportunity to wrestle.

"If I don't get knocked out first," he thought.

He sagged through more punches until one finally got him in the stomach. Lamplighter went down to one knee.

"You are getting in that van," shouted the other goon.

The shot to the gut gave the two goons the opportunity to drag the 250-pound Lamplighter away.

He then heard two shots coming from a gun. As he felt the grip of the goons give way,

Lamplighter dropped down to his stomach. He removed his hood and crawled back to his feet to see Mitch the bus driver aim his gun toward the back of the parking lot.

"I waited two years for New York State to give me a gun permit," he said. "I would say they made the correct choice."

Lamplighter then heard a yell. He turned to see two more goons trying to get Meyer into the van.

"Hey!" he yelled as the other of Vic's charges charged him.

A one-on-one fight is normally a win for Lamplighter, but this was not going to be that type of battle as Daniel, Wheeler and the co-workers rushed out of the restaurant. Seeing that he was outnumbered, the assailant aimed his gun, only to be struck down by Mitch. The remaining goon jumped into the van and sped off, leaving Professor Meyer on the concrete.

"One guess as to who sent them," Lamplighter said as Daniel and Wheeler helped him to a chair that was brought out by one of the restaurant employees.

"Good aim man," Lamplighter said to Mitch.

"A veteran and prison guard," replied Mitch as soon as the police and EMTs arrived. "Talking to these people, however, is the hard part."

He was right - he was in the lot for two more hours of police questions and medical exams.

Meyer refused to be taken to the hospital and was picked up by his wife. Canandaigua police gave Lamplighter a ride back to the apartment and promised several extra patrols of the apartment complex.

They arrived just as Gloria was returning back from her job.

"OK, what's going on here?" she nervously asked.

Don explained everything as they watched the news together. Fortunately the arrest of the ringleaders in the riots left Victor peaceful, but the Salvation Army bell ringer attacker was still on the loose.

"Well," said Gloria as she sat back in her chair. "At least we don't have to go back there again."

Knowing that they would get to sleep at different times, the couple decided to do their random Bible study earlier. He landed on John chapters 12 and 13, which told of the events surrounding the last supper.

"Now," replied Don. "I still have to go upstairs and get my work done."

Don did not have time to make any phone calls, but luckily some of the information he needed arrived via email. Don sent an email to the Victor News Editor explaining that he would only have three stories - Farmington, the Victor riots, and the plan for a new election.

He got busy working, editing the Farmington story in less than an hour. Thanks to emails from both attorney Connors and Councilman Cooper and a voice message from the acting town clerk, he was able to put together an article explaining how Victor would choose its next government.

"Why not," he thought as he grabbed the house phone for a call to Sheriff Cornell.

Cornell answered giving him the final piece to write the story on the arrest of the student and the rest of the Victor riots. He made sure to include the comments from Clive.

After finishing that, Don translated the interview from Meyer, which brought up a question.

"Why would the nephew start riots in the village where his aunt was the mayor?" Don thought as he tossed a Koosh ball back and forth.

He started working on the GEI story despite the fact that it was now 2:30 a.m. Don called up the list of individual members and found not only Mayor Watson, but Roger Shawn.

"Looks like I have a little bit more digging to do," he said. "OK - maybe a lot."

Chapter 34

Steve Clive was relaxed for his interview with the TV news channel.

"I told you it wasn't us," he said from George Donaldson's porch.

The Citizens Against The Tax maintained its 24-hour vigil in downtown Victor throughout the riots, fires and rock throwing.

"I don't know who those guys were or why they were doing here," said Clive as he leaned off of his chair into the microphone. "But I think we are redeemed with this evening's arrests."

He was joined on the porch with his wife Edith, Donaldson and a young couple from Rochester who came down after studying GEI and arrived to help protest the organization.

"It was terrible what happened here," added Edith. "We never wanted this to happen to Victor."

The reporter, a taller woman who was interviewing the group for the first time, played devil's advocate.

"But it brought attention to your movement," she said. "That is good for you."

Donaldson chimed in. "Look around you," he said. "This is not good for us."

The camera man took a look around the city at the buildings that were still boarded up. In the background were members of the Victor Department of Public Works picking up garbage.

"What is bad for this village is bad for our group," added Clive. "We want what is best for our village. Getting rid of that sustainability tax is good for our village. These riots are not."

A car pulled into Donaldson's driveway just as the news crew left.

"Hi, I'm Randall Meyer," said the Professor as he approached and offered a handshake to Clive. "I have something to discuss with you."

The report was cut and ready for the 11 p.m. news.

"Well at least it started out with some good news for us," said Donaldson as he went indoors to watch with his wife.

Absalom was glued to the news, as he always was at this time of night.

"Well, what do you guys think?" he asked his top captains.

"I don't know if this worked or not," replied Madame Stephanie. "We got rid of that stupid

Victor Town Council, but did we do enough to discredit the citizens?"

"That is the question," noted Steve. "This is more of my arena. I know that the voters can easily be manipulated, but I don't know if this was enough to get what the international organization wanted."

Julius spoke up as he leaned back in his chair.

"This is a win for us," he noted. "We proved that we could do our role. It was other people that failed."

"True," noted Absalom as he leaned back in his chair and interlocked his hands. "We did prove a point."

The second news story was a report on the Canandaigua shooting. The anchor person admitted that they had no footage, but put up photos of Lamplighter and Meyer as she described the scene based on witness accounts and the police report.

Vic entered the room and was immediately shot six times by Absalom.

"Well, one of us failed," he said as he looked around at the rest of the captains. "Now we have to get this guy into the incinerator."

The news segment prompted a call from Isadore.

"It looks like your effort to put a stop to Meyer and Lamplighter did not work," said Isadore in a stern tone. Absalom looked down at the dead Vic.

"I took care of that," replied Absalom.

"I don't care about what you do to protect your organization," yelled an irate Isadore. "I want to know what you can do to protect mine."

The newscast now led to a story about Glass and his two thefts earlier in the day.

"I've got a back-up plan," replied Absalom. "This is why I use a policy of not physically attacking outsiders. It only comes back to haunt you. He didn't listen."

Chapter 35

Don Lamplighter gave himself a busy Christmas Eve morning by his lack of sleep the night before.

"Still no clue why that riot was started," he thought to himself as he checked to make sure that the cat was fed. "I learned a lot but not enough."

Seeing that Gloria had put TK's food down earlier in the morning, he started making his bowl of cereals. For this morning he chose Raisin Bran with Fruit Loops. Lamplighter's thoughts were still rambling as he poured the milk.

"Why would a nephew start a riot in the town where his aunt was the mayor?" he asked himself for the 100 th time since he started working on the stories last night.

His bowl full, Lamplighter grabbed a banana and headed upstairs to his spare room/office to get back to work. His traditional schedule for writing stories has him getting all of the copy written by Friday night and waking up around 11 a.m. on Saturday morning for the final proof reading before sending the articles off for the Sunday deadline. The editors of all of the publications for which he worked then send him text messages while he was working his 2 p.m. to 11 p.m. shift at Wal-Mart. Lamplighter then made any necessary changes Saturday night. If he did it right, it left him time to go to church on Sunday, followed by another day at the store.

"OK, let's get going," he said as he fired up his computer.

All of last night's work changed the schedule. An exhausted Lamplighter finally fell asleep at 5 a.m. He decided to give himself more zzzz's by setting his alarm for 12:30 p.m. Lamplighter multi-tasked by chowing down on his breakfast while making the final edits.

Lamplighter applied his four-part editing method to the Farmington Town Board story. First he read the story aloud, then did a fact check, followed that by running it through the spell checker and finally gave it one more read.

The story was just a glorified listing of the minutes led by some comments about a special lighting district. He sent it off at 1 p.m.

"Cutting it pretty close," he said.

Lamplighter next went through the election story. This was pretty short and straight-forward. He sent it at 1:10.

"One more to go," he said as he opened the riots file.

Lamplighter made several changes during each of the four steps, he wrote the article starting with the arrest of A.J. Fephi followed by a chronological rehashing of events. Lamplighter added quotes from Mayor Watson, Clive, Councilman Cooper and Sheriff Cornell. It was sent at 1:37 p.m.

Lamplighter then took a quick shower and hurried to get dressed for work. He dashed out the door by 1:50 p.m. to meet Gloria, who took a break from her job across town to pick him up.

She hustled him to Wal-Mart in time for the couple to share a peck on the lips and get Don to the time clock by 2:02 p.m., barely within the allotted 5-minute grace period for starting a shift.

"Made it, thanks" he said in a text to Gloria before donning his earpiece and making way to the seasonal area.

Lamplighter spent the first two hours of his shift strictly on the register due to the influx of last minute Christmas Eve shoppers. He didn't bother to count how many he had, but he managed to say "Merry Christmas" to every one of them.

"Wow I need this," he said as he sat next to Mike the greeter during his break.

"Busy out there I take it," he responded.

"Busy day," retorted Lamplighter "I had three stories to send, plus this and a concert tonight."

Lamplighter put down his coffee and grabbed some cookies that someone had donated to the room.

"You're right," said Mike. "You do need that, since I heard that you have not played one of your relaxing games of chess this week."

"You know you are right," replied Lamplighter, followed by a sip of coffee.

He got to the room for his 15-minute break during the sports and weather of the news, and did find the Rochester paper's story on the Victor riots. That reminded him to check his cell phone for messages from editors. The only one on the list was from Gloria.

"Welcome - Merry Christmas" was the reply.

The next two hours were more of the same for Lamplighter and the rest of the Wal-Mart employees with all of the time spent on the register. Wal-Mart closed at 6 p.m. on Christmas Eve. He was the senior associate in the seasonal department and started the shut-down procedure. Lamplighter and the rest of the night crew then searched for any straggling customers before shutting down the store for good at 6:30 p.m.

Lamplighter got a text that his ride was ready. He hurried as fast as his bad leg would allow to

the front door to a vehicle driven by Captain Irving and containing two other band members.

Lamplighter was taken back to his townhouse where he changed into a white dress shirt and navy blue pants and tie before the quartet headed across town to a large community church for the annual concert.

Chapter 36

The dapperly dressed Lamplighter and the other three band members got to the largest non-denominational church in the city just as the concert was starting.

The show presented a unique format as eight churches from around Ontario County sent one of its musical performances, each of which did two songs. The final was a combined choir made up of members from all of the churches. The audience consisted of the acts that were not performing and anyone else from the community that wanted to attend. In between there were songs for the entire audience and Bible verses that were read by leaders from the eight churches.

Lamplighter and his group sneaked into their seating row during the first song for the audience.

"Just in time," said Captain Irving.

"That is what I get for working for a living," sighed Lamplighter.

The first act was a choir from a non-denominational church in Bloomfield. It was followed by a children's group from a small group that meets by rotating between people's homes in

Canandaigua. The Methodist Church in Honeoye sent a worship team consisting of two electric guitars, a keyboard player, a drummer and three singers.

Lamplighter heard a familiar voice in the middle of the song.

"Made it Sweetie," said Gloria as he took a seat behind her husband after closing her store for the holiday night.

"Good timing," replied Don. "We are up next."

The band's rendition of "Carol of the Bells" was executed well enough to draw praise from the audience.

Don took a seat next to Gloria up until the final numbers.

"That was great," she whispered into his ear. Don replied by giving her a kiss on the cheek.

Following the band was a traditional choir from a community church in Shortsville and a seniors' choir representing an independent church in Rushville.

Pastor Ben Garey from a small church in Victor took the microphone and noted that they were going to spend Christmas Eve caroling and cleaning up the village. The leaders then put on a musical performance of acoustical guitar.

"We are going to that aren't we?" asked Gloria.

"Of course," replied Don, "but we are still going to have our traditional pizza."

The host church's 40-member choir was the final act before the combined choir. Don joined that group for the singing of "O Come All Ye Faithful."

Don made a beeline for Pastor Garey to arrange the Lamplighters' visit later that night. Gloria drove the couple home. They got through the front door to find the sliding glass back door smashed open.

Gloria called 911 as Don grabbed the baseball bat that the couple keeps by the door with the intent of checking the rest of the house. He only got as far as the stairs before he ducked at a tire iron being swung at his head.

Don lifted his bat up in defense of another swing and disabled his attacker via a kick to the knee.

The smallish masked young man doubled over, allowing Don to connect with a right cross to the face. His attacker fell down knocked out.

The Lamplighters each grabbed an arm and dragged him into the living room. Don estimated that he outweighed his foe by a good 100 pounds so he sat on him while Gloria took off the mask to reveal the face of Jacob Glass.

"Well it looks like somebody finally caught you," he said as Glass started to wake up.

Two Canandaigua city police arrived. One took Glass into custody as the other drew his gun to sweep the house. All the officer found was a broken computer monitor.

A search of Glass produced some of the Lamplighter's knick-knacks.

"Curious that he didn't take any Christmas presents," said one of the officers.

"Since he went after the computer I would say somebody somewhere wants to stop me from writing," replied Don. "Too late, my stories for the week are already sent."

Don went through yet another series of police witness interviews while Gloria made some phone calls. Pastor Garey understood that the couple was going to be late for the Victor church's schedule. John the townhouse maintenance man promised to arrive to put pieces of plywood covering the windows. The police left a half hour later exchanging Christmas greetings. The city repeated its promise to increase patrols in the complex.

John arrived 15 minutes after that. In the meantime Gloria heated up the pizza that she got from the Dominos franchise that is in the same strip mall as her store. The Lamplighters shared two slices with John as they helped him put up the plywood.

"We keep these in the shed just in case," noted John as they finished their work.

TK felt safe enough to come out for her nightly feeding after John left. The Lamplighters gave her dinner before getting dressed, filling bottles with hot chocolate and taking off for Victor. It was 11:30 p.m., but Pastor Garey assured them that his church would still be both cleaning and celebrating when they arrived.

"Wal-Mart, Salvation Army and cold weather," said Gloria as they left the parking lot.

Don gave three incorrect guesses by the time they reached the city limits.

"Ah - Three different changes of clothes I wore today," he said.

"Merry Christmas," was Gloria's reply.

Chapter 37

The Lamplighters showed up at the small church where they were thinking of parking Thursday night in Victor. Only one space remained in the lot as Gloria pulled into it. Don was looking forward to a fun and relaxing midnight service until he saw the black limo parked on the street.

"Welcome," said the cheerful Garey as he was greeting visitors to the foyer just before the impromptu ceremony. "You missed the cleaning and caroling, but we have a fun service planned for tonight."

Garey walked Don and Gloria into the chapel.

"Look we even have two seats saved for you," the pastor said as he pointed to an empty spot at the end of a pew and an off-duty Sheriff Cornell waiting for them.

Don surveyed the overcrowded chapel as the couple made their way through the sanctuary.

In the first row they passed sat Mayor Watson with Councilman Cooper. On the other side of the center aisle from them sat Absalom with a man Don did not recognize. Sitting one row up from them was the Donaldson family. In front of Watson and Cooper was the Clive family. The Lamplighters sat one row up from them. Don recognized some others in the congregation from town as he reached

Sheriff Cornell. He caught a glimpse of Happy Evans and exchanged a wave before Don took his seat.

Pastor Garey continued to the altar.

"Welcome and thank you for your efforts this Christmas Eve," he said before offering a prayer.

The service began with traditional Christmas music accompanied by the church organist. The Lamplighters enjoyed singing "O Little Town of Bethlehem", "Away In A Manager" and another rendition of "Silent Night."

Garey read the account of the birth of Christ. He then invited the congregation to sing more songs. He picked "Hark! The Herald Angels Sing" and "O Come All Ye Faithful".

That was followed by an open prayer session. Garey started off by noting that the Lamplighters arrived at the service when they did because their house was broken into and the computer monitor smashed.

The mention brought a grin to Absalom's face.

That was followed by Clive, who prayed for the peace in the village and Donaldson who offered thanks for this community coming together. Cooper added a request for a positive new year.

Since nobody else spoke, Carey added a closing statement before leading the group in a chorus of "It Came Upon a Midnight Clear," then invited everyone to the fellowship hall for a hot chocolate reception.

The Lamplighters decided to mingle, but to Don's chagrin, Absalom who was parading as

Knight, was the first to speak to them.

"Sorry about your house," he said as Don put a tight grip on Gloria's hand.

"Yeah it is strange to have your house ransacked in between two church services," he replied.

"Luckily I had sent out my stories this morning."

Evans jumped in.

"You know I just got my brother a new computer for Christmas," he said. "How would you like the old monitor?"

"Merry Christmas," added Gloria. "We can pick it up after the reception."

The Donaldsons and the Clives were discussing their plans for tomorrow. Don explained that he had church in the morning while Gloria added that both of their stores would be closed so they planned to spend a quiet day at home.

Don saw Absalom leaving and let out a huge sigh of relief.

"That guy is a monster," he whispered to Gloria. "I'm glad he's gone."

The couple headed for a hot chocolate refill at the same time as Mayor Watson.

"I heard you two will be alone," she said. "Why don't you come to the family farm?"

Watson explained that she has seven siblings, each with their own farm on the outskirts of the village, but still within the town. Every Christmas they get together at their father's farm and the gathering usually drew close to 100 people.

"I appreciate the offer but we want to have a quiet day together," responded Don. "But it does sound like a great gathering."

They exchanged Christmas greetings. Gloria located Evans and motioned for Don to head outside to go to his house for the monitor. Don let out another sigh of relief as his search for the black limo proved to be fruitless.

The three went into Evans's house.

"You realize you are helping the competition," said Don as he grabbed the monitor.

"I'm helping a friend," replied Evans.

Don held the monitor in one hand and used the other to grip Evans's handshake offering.

Gloria responded in kind.

"Merry Christmas," the trio simultaneously shouted as the Lamplighters left the house.

Don and Gloria listened to Christmas music as they drove home. Gloria pointed out a farm house that still had its decorations on.

"That is pretty," she said. "It reminds me of the great gathering that the mayor is going to have tomorrow. Every member of their family owns a farm."

Don drummed his fingers on the dashboard.

"That's it," he exclaimed. "The sustainability tax takes money from large estates in the village and pays farmers that do not develop their land. The mayor's relatives are going to make a killing off of this."

"Wow," added Gloria.

"Clive and his group were protesting the tax," continued Don. "So Watson's nephew starts the riot to discredit them. The tax stays and Watson makes money."

"How does that explain Monday's shooting?" Gloria asked as they reached the Canandaigua town line.

Don thought for a second.

"Mayor Watson and Sherman, the shooter, are both part of GEI, an environmental group," he answered. "Sherman must have infiltrated the citizen's group and shot people in their name, again to keep the tax in place."

Don shrugged.

"The worst part," he added. "Is that the mobster guy's bodyguard shot him so we will never get to talk to him about it."

"Probably shot to cover it up," noted Gloria.

"Good catch," said Don. "Come Monday morning I have another story to write."

Gloria waved to the police officer on patrol in the townhouse complex as Don carried the monitor into the house.

TK greeted them as they got into their warm home. Don went straight upstairs, hooked up his gifted monitor and sent an email explaining his theory to the Victor editor.

He came down stairs for what was now Christmas Day kiss.

"Oh look," said Gloria as she turned on the TV after their encounter, "another Christmas movie."

Gloria again thumbed through for the night's Bible verse. She wound up on John Verses 4 and 5, which told the story of Christ and the woman at the well.

They played an enjoyable hour of triples before finally dozing off together.

Chapter 38

"How did *Scrooge* say it?" said the voice on the other end of the phone on Christmas morning as

Absalom sat down for breakfast. "Bah Humbug! You are supposed to be the brilliant planner and you failed."

"No I didn't," replied the banker while pouring maple syrup on his smiley-faced breakfast of bacon and eggs.

Charles Isadore leapt out of his chair, still clutching his phone.

"How dare you say that," he screamed, "our plan completely failed."

Absalom didn't even bother to stop chewing for his calm and quick reply.

"No it didn't," he repeated.

Isadore put the phone down, pounded on his desk and stomped around the room. He glared at the phone with his hands on his hips, then stomped his foot.

"How can you say that!" exclaimed Isadore into his now activated speaker phone. "We are completely exposed. You let that Lamplighter guy beat you again."

Absalom coolly took a gulp of milk then wiped his face.

"No he didn't," he said again. "People think he beat me, but he actually hasn't."

"Explain," demanded Isadore.

Absalom took a gulp of orange juice,

"See, in June he solved the murder from the train accident, but didn't connect it to me," explained Absalom. "The pastor killed himself and we got the gathering off without a hitch. Two wins for me."

"Yes I was at that party," replied Isadore who calmed down for a bit. "I agree that it was a win for us."

"Then in July, we rigged a child abduction to help us sell RFID chips," continued Absalom.

"He caught the leader of the real ring, but we are still struggling to fill the demand for the chips as people across the country are wanting them implanted."

"And since we want to track everybody it's a win for us," interrupted Isadore. "But we lost this

one."

"No we didn't," chirped Absalom with a grin.

Isadore picked up a small metal globe off of his desk and threw it across the room, nearly hitting his girlfriend in the face.

"He is going to write a story about GEI and tell everything about us," screamed Isadore.

"Everything. The riots across the country will be exposed and we lost our plan for martial law."

"Not me," Absalom sighed. "Not me ... you. You are ruined. "

There was three minutes of silence until Isadore sat back down in his chair. "What do you mean?" he asked.

Absalom stretched out his hands and cracked his knuckles.

"I come out the hero in all of this," he said during a yawn. "Think about it."

Absalom started to watch a Sunday morning news program during Isadore's second three minute silent interlude. It mentioned how much calmer the other cities were under martial law and that a recent poll showed that the people were in favor of using the National Guard. He grinned.

"Polls say that people are in favor of every part of our plan," he thought. "Now we have to ramp it up a bit."

Isadore got up again, pounded his fist into his padded chair and let out an unintelligible scream.

"OK why don't you explain it to me?" Isadore quietly said through gritted teeth.

"Your guy shot up the town council on Monday. He's connected to GEI, that made you the villain," explained Absalom. "My bodyguard shot him. That makes me, or at least Ken Knight the hero."

There was more silence as Absalom pulled out the morning paper.

"Look at this," he said. "That paper has a photo of me throwing away some garbage into a dumpster in downtown Victor last night. Again – me - hero."

Absalom turned to the jump page of the story and found another photo of the riots from

Thursday night. He explained to Isadore what it looked like.

"Again – you - zero," he said. "It gets worse for you because Jacob Glass was captured in

Lamplighter's house and we told him he was working for you. That is what he is going to tell the cops, of course he thinks it's the truth."

Absalom took a bite of bacon and continued.

"See your problem was that you made a big scene when you shouldn't have," he noted. "You would have won had you just continued with your lies and disinformation campaign instead of starting false-flag riots."

Isadore grunted as he put his head in his hands.

"You have to kill Lamplighter for me," replied Isadore. "That is the only way out of this for me."

"You succeeded in putting martial law in people's minds, but other than that, you have no way out," replied Absalom. "Other reporters are going to figure this out around the world, and besides, I have a policy, I don't kill people outside of our organization; it attracts too much attention."

"Well," replied Isadore who sat back down on the chair behind his desk, "I will find someone to kill him."

Absalom took another swig of milk.

"See that's the thing," he replied. "I do have a policy of killing people in the organization when they fail."

Absalom smiled when he heard gun shots.

Isadore's now ex-girlfriend cried after putting two bullets through his former lover's head.

Isadore now laying on the ground spotted his emergency defense pistol, which was attached to the bottom of his desk and returned fire. The two leaders of the environmental group lay dead facing each other.

Absalom grinned again.

Chapter 39

The Lamplighters had gotten ready to go to church when they got a phone call.

"Well Don," said his father "Merry Christmas, I was getting worried about you."

"Thanks, Gloria and I were getting worried about us too," Don replied. "We were attacked in our own home."

"Really, I didn't hear about that," said Lamplighter's father.

"It probably didn't make national news," noted Don.

"No," said his father "The riots did though. I guess you covered them."

"Covered them and then stopped them," noted Don, who then explained the situation to his family.

He exchanged several Christmas greeting with family members before finally hanging up 45 minutes after the call started.

Lamplighter then grabbed a cup of cocoa and headed outside toward an awaiting patrol car.

"For you," said Don as he handed the officer a hot treat. "Merry Christmas"

"Thanks," the officer replied. "I took the morning patrol, thought I would check on you."

Don took the opportunity to further explain his theory about Mayor Watson and her connections to the riots. They both agreed to investigate before parting ways with Christmas greetings.

"Either myself or other law enforcement will be back," added the officer.

"Then I should have more cocoa ready," replied Lamplighter.

Gloria made her traditional Christmas meal called 'the sampler,' which consisted of one pancake, one egg, one serving of hash browns, one glass of milk and one donut for each of them. Don contributed by reaching the cooking utensils that were on higher shelves.

"Thank you tall person," said Gloria before kissing her husband.

The couple exchanged Christmas presents after breakfast. Their economic circumstances limited their gift giving to three presents each, two of which must be practical. Don had purchased a new baking dish and a pair of gloves for Gloria. In turn, Gloria gave Don a box with one package each of underwear and socks.

Gloria opened her fun gift first. Don smiled as she pulled out a wooden mantle clock for her favorite collection.

"I wanted this one," she shouted while bouncing in her chair.

Gloria started a quiet chant as Don picked up his gift.

"Please don't have this one. Please don't have this one," she repeated as Don took off the wrapping, opened the box and found the same purple die-cast car he had been eyeing all week.